TORI MITCHELL

Coming Home to Sunset Cove

Sixth Street Books

Copyright © 2024 by Tori Mitchell

All rights reserved.

No part of this publication may be reproduced, distributed, or transmitted in any form or by any means, including photocopying, recording, or other electronic or mechanical methods, without the prior written permission of the publisher, except as permitted by U.S. copyright law.

This is a work of fiction. All characters, places, and events are products of the author's imagination or used in a fictitious manner. Any resemblance to actual persons (living or deceased) is coincidental.

Books written by Tori Mitchell

The Sunset Cove Series
Coming Home to Sunset Cove
Second Chances in Sunset Cove
Hometown Hero in Sunset Cove
Christmas in Sunset Cove
Finding Home in Sunset Cove

**Sunset Cove Shorts
(July 2025 novellas)**
The Christmas Inheritance
The Christmas Gift
The Christmas Surprise

Chapter One

Avery

Avery Brown eased her car off the highway and onto the road that would take her to Sunset Cove. She'd made the trip from Philadelphia to southern New Jersey in record time, fueled by anger and light traffic.

She glanced back at her daughter with a sad smile. Sophia looked so peaceful while she slept. It hadn't been a peaceful month, but things were about to change.

Avery pulled up her phone's Bluetooth and called her brother, Brad. He answered on the second ring.

"I'm almost home," she said. "I'm a few blocks from the house."

"Good. How was the drive?"

"No traffic. Sophia's upset, though. She fell asleep as we crossed into Sunset County."

Her brother sighed. "Of course she's upset. She's six. She doesn't understand why you had to leave. How are you holding up?"

Avery considered the question. Three days ago, her husband had announced he was in love with his secretary. He promised a fast and easy divorce, as long as she took Sophia and didn't ask for money. A clean break for everyone.

His request stung. Avery had given up her own career to support his rise in the business world, staying home with their daughter and planning social events instead of earning her own income.

So how was she holding up? Avery wasn't sure. For now, she was surviving on coffee and optimism. "I'm upset, too. I'm done with men. You can't rely on them, and you can't trust them. No offense, Brad."

This earned a laugh from her brother. "Don't bring me into this. Eric's a rotten husband, but we're not all bad."

She bit back a snarky remark. The past didn't matter. She had Sophia, and they were going to live in Sunset Cove. They would build a new life there.

Avery had been raised in the small seaside town by her grandfather after their parents died. It was a good place to grow up. "Maybe you're right, but it's time for a break. I need to do what's best for Sophia."

"Take all the time you need. I'm glad our house was waiting for you."

Avery sighed as regret washed over her. "I should have visited town while he was still alive."

Her grandfather had died last year, leaving their childhood home to her and Brad. Avery hadn't set foot in her hometown since high school. Her husband couldn't leave the office long enough to visit Sunset Cove—or maybe he just couldn't leave his secretary.

"You let Grandpa visit you, even when Eric didn't want company. That counts for something," her brother said. "Besides, you need a safe place to live with Sophia. Grandpa would want you to move back. He always hoped we'd come home, eventually."

Avery took a deep breath as the first familiar landmarks came into view. They drove by the old high school and the town hall. The Sunset Cove lighthouse stood proudly over it all.

I'm back now, she thought, closing her eyes as she waited for a red light to change. *I can't change the past, but I can start over today.*

A tear fell down Avery's cheek as she turned onto Ocean Drive and their childhood home came into view. "Oh, Grandpa. What happened to your house? Brad, this isn't good."

While the old Victorian home was still beautiful, it had lost its shine. The siding needed a fresh coat of paint. Weeds choked out her grandfather's flower garden. Someone had mowed the lawn, but the yard was filled with more weeds than blades of grass.

"Is it that bad?" Brad asked. "I visited Grandpa before he passed. The house was getting shabby, but it was solid."

She stopped to consider the property. The porch looked sturdy. The roof was in good shape. Maybe Brad was right. If the house had good bones, they would be fine.

The home had been in their family for decades, purchased long before beach properties became popular. It had been moved into town from the edge of the sea, away from the eroding shoreline and punishing waves.

Just like Avery, the house had gotten a second chance.

Their home had lost its first floor to flooding before being moved to its current location. Avery could relate—she'd also been gutted, transplanted, and expected to stand strong without her missing pieces.

Still, she was grateful for the soft landing. She'd loved living close to the ocean, and there was no way she could afford a home in Sunset Cove now.

Avery parked her car in the driveway and said goodnight to her brother. While her daughter had slept through the phone call, she woke to the sound of tires crunching over a shell driveway.

"Are we there yet?" Sophia asked, her words slurring with sleepiness. "I want to see the ocean. I've never seen the ocean."

Avery gathered her daughter in her arms. "The ocean will be there tomorrow. Let's get some sleep first."

A full moon lit the way as she carried her daughter up the porch steps. She shimmied the key in the lock and opened the creaky front door. Her stomach dropped as they walked across the threshold. Sheets protected the furniture, but one of the side windows was cracked. Dusty carpet muffled her footsteps on the stairs up to her old room.

She pulled the sheet off her bed, then laid her daughter onto a mattress that hadn't been touched since she moved out a decade ago.

"It's dusty, but nothing we can't clean up. It's better than the mess we left behind," she whispered, giving her daughter a gentle kiss on the forehead.

Avery pulled out a blanket from the chest at the foot of the bed. The blanket was blessedly clean, so she used it to tuck in her daughter and closed the door.

In the kitchen, she pulled a chair from its perch on the table and turned it upright. Then she sunk her head onto the table and cried.

How did I get here? she asked herself. *Where do I go from here?*

After a few minutes of self-pity, she wiped away her tears and gathered her bags from the car. She pulled out a notepad and pen and started a list. There was lots to do, but taking care of Sophia was her top priority. Her daughter needed to go to school, there was no food in the house, and Avery needed a job to pay for it all. She'd fix the window and start the furnace, too.

One step at a time. Things would look better in the morning. At least, she hoped they would look better.

She went out onto the porch and sat quietly, listening to the ocean crash against the nearby shore.

This was a new town, a new house, and a new life. Avery was determined to make the most of their second chance.

Chapter Two

Grant

Grant threw his toolbox into the back of his truck and climbed into the driver's seat. It would be another long day. Not a problem. There was no shame in long hours and hard work.

The sun was rising when he pulled onto the job site. His construction company had just started on the O'Neill house, a beachfront beauty that was too small for its current owners. They'd spend the next few weeks here building a new bedroom suite and a kid-friendly area upstairs.

His foreman, Nick Butler, greeted him as walked through the door. "Hey, boss. How's it going?"

Grant grunted and glanced around at the mess they'd made for the sake of progress. His small crew filled the space, moving materials and planning out their day. "You tell me. Did you get the supplies we ordered?"

"It came an hour ago, while you were sleeping. I hope you got enough beauty rest." Nick grinned at his boss, then glanced down at his clipboard. "There was a small problem with the order. There's not enough drywall for the master bedroom. The supplier's blaming…"

"Supply chain issues, right?"

"You called it. We're working on the toy room while we wait for the rest of our order."

Grant slapped Nick on the back and nodded. "Good thinking. I'll work some nights and weekends once the drywall gets here. We'll meet our deadline."

Nick stopped writing for a moment, letting his pencil hover over the clipboard. Grant imagined the gears spinning in his friend's head. He braced himself, because he knew what was coming. First Nick would poke fun at him, then he would start a pep talk.

The two men had been raised in the same neighborhood. They'd been swinging hammers and exchanging jabs since elementary school. That's why Grant wasn't surprised when Nick picked humor over a lecture.

"If you didn't work all night, you might wake up on time. Besides, there are more fun things to do at night. All work and no play…" Nick punched his boss in the arm and grinned.

It wasn't easy being the owner of Grant Construction. Grant had worked long hours over the past five years, building his business and a reputation as one of the most honest companies in Sunset Cove. It was important that people trust him. Sunset Cove was his home, and it always would be.

Still, the endless days were wearing him down. Nick was right—he overslept this morning. He'd meant to be here when their shipment arrived. But their last project was running over deadline, and he'd worked until midnight finishing detail work.

Instead of joking with Nick, he grunted again and trudged back to the toolbox in his truck.

Nick crossed his arms and watched Grant stomp back to the house. "You're working too much if you can't take a joke at nine a.m. This business is important to you. It's important to me, too. But you need a life outside of work. When's the last time you took a vacation?"

Grant rolled his eyes. *Here it comes: My monthly lecture on why I should marry a woman instead of my job.* Grant couldn't argue with Nick's reasoning. The exchange still put him on the defensive. "I don't have time for a vacation right now. I don't have time for a girlfriend, either. What kind of life do you think I need?"

His friend scanned his clipboard again, ticking check marks in boxes. "I don't know. Maybe a wife and a few kids? When you find the right person, you'll make time for them. You need someone to pull you off the job and home each night."

"I like my house. Besides, not all of us are that lucky," he said, shaking his head as he slid on his tool belt and pulled the clipboard from his friend's hands. "Don't get cocky because you met a great woman."

"I am lucky," Nick said, perking up. He walked over to a makeshift table and grabbed a thermos of coffee. After a long swig, he grinned. "My wife makes me coffee every morning. I'm the luckiest guy in the world."

"You also get no sleep." Grant laughed and picked up his own thermos. "She made coffee for a reason. Isn't that why you're here at seven a.m.?"

"The day starts early when you have kids," he agreed, taking another chug of caffeine. "Besides, if I start my day early, I can leave early. I've got to pick the girls up at school today."

Grant nodded, skimming over the list in his hand. He'd make sure Nick was off the site in plenty of time, even if it meant Grant stayed later than usual. That's how it worked when you owned a business. "Let's finish the upstairs teardown. If we stay focused, we can hang the drywall we've got left and both go home early."

Grant thought about Nick's words all morning. His friend was right. He was working too many hours. Most of the time, he didn't mind. Grant loved his job and Sunset Cove. He'd grown up here and enjoyed helping to shape the town, one home or business at a time. He took pride in his work and liked seeing their completed projects as he drove through the small town.

Still, he was almost thirty. He'd wanted a family by now. Not much he could do about it, though. There wasn't sense in starting a relationship until you found the right woman. Nick was right about that, too.

More than a decade ago, he'd found the perfect partner—or so he'd thought. He'd been best friends with Avery Brown in high school. He'd felt a spark between them a time or two. Still, he'd never been brave enough to ask her out. Avery, Nick, and their friend Brook had gone everywhere together, but none of them had moved beyond friendship.

The day after graduation, Avery left their small town for college life. She'd never returned. He hadn't seen her since they were eighteen.

He wondered what Avery was doing now. Grant soon found himself daydreaming about her long, dark hair and quiet voice. He picked up a new nail and aimed his hammer at the drywall. One swing. Two swings.

"Ouch!" he yelled.

Nick came running into the room. "What's wrong?" he asked. "You okay?"

Grant stood with the hammer tucked under his arm. His left hand sported a bright red thumb. "I'm fine. I missed."

Nick burst out laughing. "You own a construction business, and can't swing a hammer? I'll find the bandages."

Grant sighed and checked his hand. He'd split his thumb open. Blood rushed out of the wound, dripping onto his good hand and making a decent-sized puddle.

Nick handed him a few paper towels, then followed him to the bathroom with the first aid kit. "What were you thinking about when you swung the hammer?"

Grant glanced sideways at his friend before holding his hand under running water. If he told Nick about Avery, his friend would never let it go. He didn't know where Avery lived now, but Nick would find her. He'd always been a matchmaker and wouldn't let distance stop him from meddling. Nick was married with three kids and thought everyone deserved the same fate.

His friend finished wrapping up his thumb, and Grant stood up. "Thanks. That's my sign to head back to the office. I've got supplies to order for next month's restaurant expansion."

"Good idea. Did you buy the candy for Halloween yet?"

Grant turned on his phone and checked the date. October 25—only a few more days until trick-or-treat night. He loved seeing the town's kids in costume and handing out candy from their Main Street office. Kids knew he had the best treats in town. They came from all over Sunset Cove to visit.

He'd been so busy this year that trick-or-treat had almost slipped his mind. Hopefully, he could find enough candy to keep the kids happy.

"I'm not ready yet, but I will be," he said. "Thanks for the reminder. I'll stop by the store on my way back."

Grant grabbed a piece of paper and scribbled out a list. Ten large bags of candy, and three packs of full bars for the best costumes. Water bottles for the parents. A few stickers and toys for the kids with food allergies. That should be enough.

Nick shook his head. "For someone without kids, you go all out."

Grant grabbed his toolbox and headed for his truck. Nick was right again, of course. He loved kids. He just hadn't found the time or woman to start a family. Maybe one day.

Chapter Three

Avery

Avery walked out of Sunset Cove Elementary School with a smile on her face. Sophia was officially enrolled in first grade. While Avery was nervous about the transition, her daughter had happily skipped off to the playground to join her new classmates. The girl's resilience amazed her. She would likely come home talking about ten new friends.

The elementary school hadn't changed much since Avery was a student. Sure, the building had a new foyer and a fresh coat of paint—but much of it looked the same. The hallways hadn't changed. She even recognized a few people sitting at the front desk.

Looking back, Avery wasn't sure why she had waited so long to come back to Sunset Cove. She should have visited her grandfather more often. Her ex-husband hadn't encouraged her to come home, but she had a car and they were only two hours away. She could have made the drive at least once a year.

She hadn't stayed in touch with her friends, either. Once she'd married Eric, it was like she'd forgotten her past life.

That time was behind her, she reminded herself. It was time to start over, and this would be a good change for Sophia. Avery had grown roots here. Now the two of them could regrow those roots together. It was a nice town filled with great people, so unlike the big city she'd left behind.

She pulled out onto Main Street and headed toward the grocery store. Sunset Market had been her favorite place to buy snacks after school with her friends. She'd be shopping for snacks today, and a lot more.

Avery pulled out her shopping list and sighed. Snacks, cleaning supplies, lunch and dinner staples. They were starting fresh in every way, and that included her empty pantry. The cash she'd brought with them wouldn't last long. Finding a job would be a top priority.

She pushed her cart down each aisle, slowly filling the cart and daydreaming as she went. When was the last time she was in this store—eight years ago? Ten years?

"It was a long time ago," she muttered. "Too long."

She'd come to Sunset Market with her friends the night of high school graduation. They'd celebrated graduation with their normal routine: chips, soda, and talking under the night sky. It had been a great night, one filled with excitement for the future. But the evening had also held a hint of sadness. They'd all known that things were about to change forever.

She shook her head, thinking about that night with Brook, Grant, and Nick. They'd all been so close. She'd hoped Grant would kiss her for the first time that night. But he hadn't. She'd left the next morning for college and never came back. That was the end of their could-have-been relationship.

Avery continued down the aisle while she looked over her list. Nearly done. She had four hours left to get home, unpack everything she'd bought, and attempt to turn her grandfather's dusty house into a home for Sophia.

Her mind was focused on her to-do list when she turned the corner and crashed into an oncoming cart.

"Whoa! Easy there!" A tall man with dark, wavy hair reached out and steadied her cart before it could topple over. "The store has a dented can discount policy, but we're not supposed to dent the cans ourselves."

He chuckled at his joke and picked up the can of green beans she'd knocked onto the floor. He set the can on the shelf, then took a good look at her face. His eyes widened in surprise. "Avery Brown? Is that you?"

Her eyes skimmed over the man, pausing at his broad shoulders before settling on his friendly face and bright green eyes. He'd grown taller and more muscular since high school, like he knew how to put in a hard day's work. His eyes were still the same, though. She'd dreamed of those eyes for weeks after leaving Sunset Cove. "Grant! What are you doing here? I didn't know you still lived in town."

He gestured to his cart filled with candy and Halloween decorations. "We're getting ready for Trick or Treat. Can't disappoint the kids. Our storefront gives out more candy than any other business on Main Street."

Her eyes widened as she mentally tallied how much candy he was buying. "I hope your own kids don't get jealous. That's a lot of sweets to hide from them."

"No kids at home. But I'll need to hide this from my co-workers," he added. "Remember Nick? He's my worst candy thief."

Avery laughed and shook her head. "I haven't heard from Nick in years. I was just thinking about our friends. I haven't seen everyone in so long."

Grant hesitated and seemed to consider his next words. After shifting his weight from one foot to the next, he nodded. "We should get everyone together. Are you in town for long?"

She thought about her daughter cheerfully running to the playground, and their old house that was waiting to be turned into a home.

"Yes, we're staying for a while," she said, gesturing vaguely toward the town where they'd both been raised. "I'd love to see everyone again. I just moved back to town with my daughter. Fresh starts and all that."

He nodded seriously. "Sometimes we need to start over in a familiar place. It's great to see you again."

The two friends exchanged phone numbers, and Grant promised to text soon. Avery started to walk away when he shouted, "Wait!"

She stopped and turned back toward him.

He leaned against the cart, looking sheepish. "We didn't end on the best note when you left. I should have stayed in touch. Can we have a fresh start too?"

Avery hesitated, surprised. Wasn't life funny? Just a few minutes ago she had been thinking of her last night with Grant, wishing that things had been different. Now he wanted to start over.

The timing wasn't ideal. She was still married until her husband signed the divorce paperwork, and she had to think about Sophia before she made any big changes. Her daughter had been through so much already. She couldn't afford to daydream about missed kisses and second chances at romance.

"I'd like a fresh start," she said, carefully choosing her words. "As friends. I just left a bad marriage, and the divorce isn't final yet."

Grant looked disappointed, but covered his disappointment with a broad smile. "Friends like coffee, right? Let's meet for coffee tomorrow. Seaside Cupcakes is just down the street," he said, pointing out the door of the grocery store. "That's Brook's place. She's got amazing coffee and the best cupcakes and muffins."

Brook Reed had been Avery's best friend. Now she owned a bakery, and Avery knew nothing about it. She hadn't spoken to her best friend since high school. Her heart sank as she realized how out of touch she was with her hometown, and how much she had missed. She should have supported her friends. Instead, she'd stayed in the city, content to build a new life and forget everyone who had loved her in the past.

Never again, she promised herself. She would be a better friend going forward. She forced a bright smile and said, "Coffee sounds good. I drop Sophia off at school at eight o'clock. Can we meet at nine?"

Avery grabbed the last few things she needed at the store. At the checkout aisle, she ran into Grant again.

"I look forward to running into each other," he said, winking at her. "But no more collisions. I'm already injured today," he said, waving his wrapped thumb.

She was still smiling when she got into her car. As she drove away, Avery realized that she hadn't laughed or smiled this much in a long time. Life had a funny way of giving you exactly what you needed.

Three hours later, Avery sat on the front porch of her grandfather's home. It had been a busy day.

The house was warm, thanks to the local hardware store owner. He'd patched the cracked window and turned on the furnace. She'd unpacked her groceries and cleaning supplies, then scrubbed the floors and walls of their new house. Now she rested on the porch, eager for her daughter's bus to arrive so she could hear about the first day of school.

The yellow bus's brakes squealed as it turned the corner and stopped in front of their house.

"Mom! Mom! I had a great day!" Sophia shouted, racing off the bus with her backpack dragging behind her. "I made four new friends. We had chicken nuggets for lunch. I like it here."

Avery gave her daughter a tight hug. She swallowed the lump in her throat and promised herself that she wouldn't cry. Her little girl was happy here, and that was all that mattered. They could get through anything together.

The six-year-old chattered happily as the two of them went into the house. One of her new friend's last names was familiar, Avery noted. Maybe she had gone to school with the child's father. These little reminders of her childhood hadn't happened in the city. She liked the reminders.

"Mmmmm. It smells good. Did you make pizza dough?" her daughter asked, dashing toward the kitchen. "It's not even Friday! Can I stretch the dough? Let's put on lots of cheese."

Avery smiled at her daughter's excitement. Pizza always made her happy. They'd had pizza Fridays back when she was married. Eric had worked late on Fridays, which meant that the two girls were home alone for dinner. Pizza was fun and hands-on. It distracted her from the fact that her husband spent too much time at work.

Now she knew why he was always gone. He'd been busy spending time with her replacement.

She brushed that thought aside and slipped Sophia's bookbag off her tiny shoulders. "I wanted something special for your first day of school. What did you learn? What was your teacher like?"

The two of them leaned their heads together as they worked the dough. Avery gazed at her daughter's face as she stretched the dough as far as her short arms would allow. Sophia's light blue eyes and blond curls reminded her so much of Eric.

But she wouldn't think about Eric tonight. Instead, her mind drifted toward another man with wavy hair. She hadn't realized

Grant was still in Sunset Cove. It shouldn't surprise her. While she'd fled town the day after graduation, looking for greener pastures, Grant had stayed to care for his handicapped mother. He'd done it with a smile, too. He knew that family came first.

Avery sighed as she watched Sophia dump handfuls of cheese on their pizza. What would life have been like if she'd stayed in Sunset Cove? She would still be in touch with her friends, and probably wouldn't have this aching loneliness. But she also wouldn't have Sophia.

She had regrets, but having Sophia wasn't one of them. It was good to be back, though. They could heal here and start over. Her daughter would be happy at the beach, and with her new friends and school.

Avery hoped to find happiness for herself, too.

Chapter Four

Grant

"Are we ready?"

"We're ready."

Nick's wife, Jessica, glanced at the bowls overflowing with candy. "I don't think we're ready. Do we have enough?"

Grant laughed. He'd gathered fifteen giant bags of candy and ten sleeves of full chocolate bars. "We've got coloring books, crayons, stickers, and toys from the dollar store. How could we not be ready?"

Jessica's eyebrows pinched together as she frowned. "You weren't here last year. Remember? You were off helping the Smith family finish some last-minute work on their house. You weren't here when fifty kids came at once, and we only had forty pieces of candy left." She shuddered. "It was horrible."

Nick wrapped his arm around his wife. "Grant's staying here, and I am too. I'm sorry we abandoned you last year. If we run out of candy, I'll go buy some more."

"Good luck with that," she muttered, straightening the parade of glow sticks that lined the edge of the table. "Every store was out of candy when I checked this morning."

Grant shook his head. He was happy to be here this year. Jessica wasn't wrong to complain. Every year he planned to hand out treats for Halloween. He looked forward to it. He loved seeing the kids' costumes and greeting the parents that he grew up with. And every year, a work emergency dragged him out of the office and into the work site.

This was the first time in four years that he'd be able to hand out treats. He'd used a red marker and blocked off the entire afternoon and evening, just to make sure that his crew would be available during trick-or-treat.

"I still don't think it's fair that you get to be the construction worker," Nick said, pointing at Grant's hard hat. "Why do I have to be the cowboy?"

"When you're the boss, you can pick out the costumes." Jessica pretended to glare at her husband. "Don't forget it was your idea to dress up as the Village People. Besides, you make a cute cowboy."

Watching his best friend and wife banter back and forth was usually fun. Today it got on Grant's nerves. He pushed himself out of the chair and began pacing up and down the sidewalk. "You might be right. We don't have enough candy. I'll see if there are snacks in our break room stash to hand out."

Grant walked back into the building. Once he was in the quiet office, he took a deep breath. What was wrong with him? He loved hanging out with Nick. Jessica was great, and their kids were amazing, too. Still, spending time with his friends' family made him realize what he was missing. Seeing Avery at the grocery store had sent him for a loop. He wondered how different things would have been if he hadn't been too afraid to ask her out when they were teenagers.

He grabbed a box filled with potato chips and carried them out to the sidewalk table. "This should do it, right?"

Jessica sighed and tucked the box under their table. "It'll help with the last-minute rush."

"So…" Nick leaned on the table and toward Grant. "How many trick-or-treaters will we get tonight? Anyone special coming?"

Grant avoided his gaze, not sure where his friend was going with this conversation. "No idea. We might get a few hundred kids. But I didn't invite anyone."

"Of course, you didn't," Nick smirked. "You've been distracted all week. Aunt Jane saw you talking to a woman at the store when you bought all this candy. Were you checking out more than treats?"

Grant rolled his eyes. It was just his luck that someone had been watching. You couldn't hide in a small town. "Oh, yeah. That was Avery Brown. Remember her from high school?" he asked, trying to spin the conversation into safer territory. "She's back home. She has a kid now. Maybe we'll see her tonight. We'll see."

"I guess we will."

Grant watched his friend nervously. Nick prided himself on his match-making skills. He'd set up half their friends in high school and still had a knack for putting new couples together. If Nick got his claws into Avery, he'd never hear the end of it.

He quietly sighed with relief as the first trick-or-treater arrived. Saved by the candy-grabbers.

Jessica gave her a piece of chocolate and a few kind words. Grant couldn't help but smile at the little girl, too. He guessed she was about the same age as Avery's girl. Any kid with Avery's genes had to be just as cute, too.

Maybe it wouldn't be such a bad thing if Nick found him a match. He knew Avery was off limits. She was only looking to be friends. If Nick found him a girlfriend, he could finally stop daydreaming about Avery Brown.

Sadly, he didn't think it would be that easy. He'd been surprised to realize he still had feelings for Avery. Just seeing her in the grocery store had pushed his thoughts back to high school. She wouldn't be an easy girl to forget.

· ♥ · ♥ · ♥ · ♥ · ♥ ·

"Come on, come on. We're going to be late," Sophia urged her mom. "I'm ready. You don't even have shoes on."

Avery rushed into the living room, brushing her hair as she went. She was glad Sophia had picked out her costume before Eric kicked them out. This week had been crazy enough without worrying about Halloween.

She looked at her daughter in her princess gown and felt anger boil to the surface. How could Eric push this perfect little girl away? Enough about Eric, she resolved, putting the hairbrush down on the counter with more force than necessary. She dashed over to the front door to grab her shoes and hopped around the foyer, putting them on. Then Avery threw on a comfortable sweater and tucked Sophia's jacket into her bag.

"Mom, let's go! Where's your costume? You always dress up, too."

Mom's costume is "a single mom who didn't have time to dress up," she thought. She saved those words for herself, though. Her daughter didn't need to know how much she was struggling. Instead, she just smiled. "We're focusing on you this year, kiddo. I didn't want to risk upstaging my princess."

Sophia seemed satisfied with that answer. She stood up a bit taller and straightened her crown. "I understand. That's a risk that we can't take. No one should shine brighter than a princess."

Avery held back a snicker as she ushered her daughter out the door. Sophia skipped down the porch steps, swinging her loot bag with big, cheerful movements. It amazed her how well her daughter was coping with so much change.

Avery knew how devastated she felt as a wife and mom. She'd put all of her effort into their marriage and family. Her entire identity had been ripped away when Eric announced their divorce. If she wasn't Mrs. Eric Goodwin, then who was she?

It was time to find out. After all, she'd been Miss Avery Brown for years before she married Eric. She'd been happy back then, too. Now it was time to find a new identity and a new kind of happiness.

Feeling slightly lighter, she walked Sophia from one neighbor's door to the next. They worked their way down one street and up another, slowly moving toward the center of town. Unless things had changed since Avery left, all the businesses on Main Street would have tables set up on the sidewalk.

"Look, mom. It's like a party," Sophia exclaimed. "Let's go!"

Avery's eyes widened as she took in the scene on Main Street. She'd gone trick-or-treating on the same roads as a kid. It hadn't even been that long ago. She'd come with her friends in high school, walking with Brook, Grant, and Nick to collect candy and other goodies. In Sunset Cove, no kid was too old to go trick-or-treating. It was just one other thing she loved about small towns.

Still, something had changed. Halloween was much, much bigger than she remembered. Or else her perspective had shifted as she'd grown taller. She just hadn't expected to see so many people out to support the town's kids.

"Look! Mom, it's mermaids," Sophia shouted, rushing to the first table. Avery smiled to see the plumber's daughters dressed as mermaids and handing out ring pops. Their dad, the same plumber her grandfather had called when he had a problem, watched over the table with a pirate patch over one eye.

"And over there, Mom! Look, they have books!" Sophia raced over to the library's table and gave a sweet smile as the town's librarian handed her a thin princess book. "This book is perfect for you, don't you think?"

Sophia nodded seriously. "I love princesses, and I love books."

"What do you say?" her mom prompted her.

"Thank you very much," Sophia said. "Mom, we don't have a library card here. Can we get one?"

The woman behind the table smiled and handed Avery a piece of paper. "You sure can! Here's the application. Bring it in at any time. Every princess needs a library card."

Avery thanked her and tucked the paper into her bag, touched by the woman's kindness. They continued on, stopping at most tables for a moment to gush over costumes and let Sophia pick out a treat.

"Mom, Mom, Mom, I found a cowboy." Avery sighed and tried to keep up with her daughter's enthusiasm. She hoped the cowboy was serving strong coffee. "He's standing next to a police officer. Let's go to that table next." Sophia grabbed her mom's hand and pulled her toward a group of people dressed as the Village People.

Avery watched as Sophia carefully picked out a piece of candy. The woman dressed as a police officer smiled at her and pushed the bowl a bit closer. "Take two pieces. It's not every day that royalty visits our table."

The cowboy came to greet them, his hat tipped low to cover most of his face. "Howdy, there. Aren't you a pretty little princess? I bet you're about twelve years old, right?"

Sophia giggled. "I'm six. But I'm tall for my age. I could see why you think I'm twelve."

Avery laughed and fluffed the blonde curls on her daughter's head. "She's six going on sixteen, that's for sure." Then she glanced up at the cowboy as he tipped back his hat. "Nick! How are you doing?"

"It's Avery, right? This is my wife, Jessica. I'll be right back, I think we're gonna run out of candy soon." He dashed inside the building.

"That was strange," Jessica said. "Then again, Nick's a strange guy. We're not running out of candy yet." She gestured toward the bowl, still filled to the brim.

Nick's motivation was clear soon enough. Moments later, he rushed out of the building with a construction worker on his heels.

"I hear we've got a special visitor here tonight," the construction worker said as he came down in front of the table and gave a deep bow. "Would Your Majesty like a chocolate bar or a coloring book? We save the best and biggest prizes for the little girls with the best costumes."

Sophia giggled, then pushed back her shoulders and did her best impression of royalty. "I decree that all candy given out on Halloween should be chocolate. Milk chocolate is best. Something with peanut butter would be good too."

"It shall be done." He pulled out a bar of chocolate peanut butter and handed it to Sophia with a flourish. "Would the queen's mother like a treat too?"

Then Grant looked past Sophia and saw Avery. He jumped to his feet, almost dropping the candy on the ground in the process. "Avery. Hi! How are you? Nick said we had a good costume out here, but he didn't tell me it was your daughter." He glanced back at Nick and gave his friend a look. "You remember each other, right?"

"Of course I do," Nick said. "You didn't want to miss the chance to see Avery or her daughter. Isn't she an adorable princess?"

"I'm adorable," Sophia said.

Jessica stifled a laugh behind her hands.

Grant didn't bother holding back his laugh. He held out a second candy bar. "She's the cutest princess I've seen today. Share this with your mom, okay?"

"Say thank you to Mr. Grant." Avery nodded as her daughter echoed her thanks. "Are you sure you'll have enough candy? You can't give out two big bars to every kid you see. What would your boss say?"

Nick looked at Grant and cocked his head. "I think our boss would be very, very upset. We should be handing out more candy. Two bars for each kid isn't enough."

Avery looked so uncomfortable that Jessica chimed in. "It's fine, honey. Grant is the boss. It's not good for his ego, but we let him do whatever he wants. Even if it does mean every kid in the county gets too much chocolate."

"You own this place?" Avery's eyes widened.

"I do. I started working in construction after high school. Then when Mom died, I got a small inheritance and started Grant Construction. I work hard, but I'm proud of what we've grown here."

Avery seemed impressed. "You should be proud. Not many people can say that they own a successful business."

Sophia grew impatient as the adults stared at each other. She tugged at her mom's coat sleeve and pointed to a clown. "They're giving out balloon animals. Could they make me a dog?"

"That clown is my friend," Nick said, nodding seriously. "Tell him to make a dog and a flower for you."

Sophia squealed and started pulling her mother away.

"Sorry about this. We'll talk later," Avery said.

"Don't forget to stop by the beach!" Grant called. "The pumpkin decorating contest is almost over. It ends tonight at dusk."

Grant sighed as they walked away. Avery's daughter was cute. She didn't look a lot like her mom, though. He wondered where Sophia's dad was and if he was still in the picture. For a moment, he let himself wonder what a girl that was his and Avery's would look like.

Then he shook his head. Enough daydreaming. Avery had a family already. He'd missed his chance.

"Earth to Grant," Nick whispered. "Avery is just as pretty as I remember. Kid's sharp as whip, too."

Grant looked at his friend and thought about Nick's epic match-making skills. He knew he had no shot with Avery, and wasn't ready to put his heart out there to get crushed. "Yeah, they both seem pretty great. Don't get any ideas. We're just friends."

Chapter Five

Avery

Avery had forgotten about the pumpkin decorating contest. Every year on Halloween night, families gathered on the beach to make sandcastles. They weren't just your average summertime castles, though. These were Halloween masterpieces. Even the chilly ocean breeze couldn't stop the locals from gathering for this tradition.

"Let's hurry up, honey. After you get your balloon, we need to go down to the beach."

Sophia clapped her hands and cheered. "I love the beach. I wish we'd always lived here."

It was a wonderful place to grow up, Avery agreed, taking her daughter's hand and swinging it as they stood in line for Sophia's balloon dog. Five minutes and ten squeaky twists of a balloon later, they were on their way.

Sophia looked into her bulging treat bag. "I have enough candy. Why don't we go to the beach now?" The little girl continued to chatter as they walked toward the shore. "Did you like growing up here? Why did you move? I like it here. I don't think we should ever leave."

Avery hesitated, then tried to answer the simplest question first. "I left to go to school, remember?"

"You went to college in the city. There aren't any colleges around here. And that's where you met Daddy."

"That's where I met Daddy," Avery agreed. Her brow furrowed as she considered how much information she should give her six-year-old daughter. "I met your dad. We got married, and then you were born."

"I like being born!"

"Your being born is the favorite part of my story."

"And then what happened?"

"Well…" She paused, staring toward the boardwalk as they continued to walk down to the beach. "And then Mommy and Daddy weren't married anymore. Grandpa gave us his house, and now we live here."

Sophia smiled. "I love a happy ending."

Avery squeezed her daughter's hand. Things always seemed better when you looked at them through a child's eyes. Was this their happy ending? She wasn't sure, but it was a lot better than sitting in Eric's house alone all day waiting for him to come home, wondering what type of mood he'd be in that day. He'd grown distant as the years went by. He'd been more worried about work and keeping up his social schedule than he was about his own wife and daughter.

Never again, she promised herself. Sophia came first in everything. It wouldn't hurt Avery to put herself on that priority list, too.

When they reached the sand, Sophia let out another shriek. "What did they do to the beach?"

Avery felt a swell of excitement as she saw the mix of teenagers, families, and even the local lifeguards on the beach. Each group was scooping and sculpting sandcastles, carefully tucking pumpkins and other spooky additions into their sandy creations.

"They're Halloween sandcastles," she explained. "It's one of my favorite fall traditions. Let's put your coat on, then you can check it out."

Sophia reluctantly shrugged into her jacket, then walked up to one of the lifeguards. She yanked her princess dress above her knees and kneeled on the sand. "Can I help you? I've never made a sandcastle before."

Avery reached for her daughter's hand. "Sweetheart, let's go make our own. Let this boy build his own castle."

The boy, who couldn't have been more than sixteen years old, just smiled. "It's okay, I've got two younger sisters. They're busy trick-or-treating. I'd love to have help from a princess. Every princess knows what a castle should look like."

Sophia nodded. "I am very familiar with castles," she said, sliding back into character. "Let's build lots of towers where the princess can lean out the window and watch over her kingdom. But they need to be spooky castles. It's Halloween! We can't forget to make it spooky."

He laughed and handed her a bucket. "I'm Jack. If it's okay with your mom, why didn't you go down and get me a bucket of water? The sand is too dry. It needs to be wet enough to stay together when I use the molds."

Avery smiled warmly at Jack and watched as her daughter scrambled to stand up and grab the bucket. Together, mother and daughter carried the bucket of water back to Jack's area.

Jack patiently showed Sophia how to mix some water with the sand and scoop it into the molds. He tapped the first mold to settle the sand, then flipped it over.

"It's a tower." Her eyes grew wide. "I love it. Can we make another one?"

Avery watched as the two children worked together to build a complex structure with more towers than any of the other sandcastles. As the sun began to set, Jack carefully scratched a hole in a few of the towers and slid in battery-powered candles.

Then they stood back and watched as the judges examined each creation. There were about twenty castles on the beach, each lit in some way. Some used batteries. Others held real candles and flames. Each one was beautiful. Their lights shimmered and reflected on the waves crashing just beyond the castles.

Avery felt her phone vibrate. She glanced at the screen and saw that it was her lawyer calling. *Not now*, she thought, sliding the call straight to voicemail. She didn't want to miss the best part of the sand castle competition.

Avery's favorite part of the tradition was the judging. Every group earned an award. Together, Jack and Sophia were awarded a prize for the "most fit for a princess" castle. Sophia beamed as she accepted her prize—a small sand bucket filled with a shovel, rake, and tiny crab mold.

"It's my first sand bucket," she yelled, making all the judges laugh. "Now I can build sand castles every day."

"We might not build too many castles in the winter, but we'll come here on the next warm day," her mom promised. They thanked Jack for sharing his time and began the walk back toward town.

The two of them ambled back to their new home in silence. Avery was filled with a sense of contentment that she hadn't felt in a long time. It was good to see her daughter doing the same thing she had done as a child. She hadn't minded living in the city. But now that she was back in Sunset Cove, she knew it was where they were meant to be.

"It's almost bedtime," she told her daughter. "Let's sort some candy and then get ready for bed. Tomorrow is a school day."

Sophia rushed toward the kitchen table and emptied her loot bag. She pulled out a few pieces of dark chocolate and set them aside. "You can have this candy. These are your favorite."

Avery settled onto the kitchen chair and watched her daughter sort through her candy. She was a generous kid, always willing to share.

As Sophia made two piles to keep or share, Avery let her mind wander. What would life have been like if she'd stayed in Sunset Cove? She could have met a nice guy. Nicer than Eric, that's for sure. They'd have bought a house not too far from the beach.

In her dream marriage, she would have more than one child by now. Eric hadn't wanted children at all. Sophia had been a welcome surprise for Avery, but not so much for Eric. If she'd stayed in Sunset Cove, Sophia might be a master sand castle artist by now. She'd have a little brother or sister to teach, just like Jack.

Instead of celebrating Sophia's first week at Sunset Cove Elementary, it would be Avery's second year on the PTO. She'd know every school teacher and spend lots of time in the school volunteering.

Maybe her husband would have a business that she could help run.

She snapped out of her daydream when she realized that Grant was in every picture: his children, his sandcastles, and his business.

That wasn't going to happen. Even when she was ready to start dating again, it would be tough to find someone interested in dating a single mom. Sophia was a good kid, but a lot for a new boyfriend to take on. She suspected that most men wouldn't be interested in her once they realized that Sophia was part of a package deal.

She needed to be careful. She couldn't let random dates wander into their lives. It would be too confusing for Sophia if men came and left too often.

Still, Grant knew about her daughter. She'd mentioned her the first time they met. It hadn't stopped him from asking to meet for coffee. She wouldn't get her hopes up, though. They were just friends. Coffee was a chance to catch up. Nothing more.

As Sophia finished her candy sorting, Avery left her daydreaming behind and moved back into mom mode. She sent her daughter down the hallway for a bath and grabbed her to-do list. First thing tomorrow, she would call back her lawyer. Then she needed to find a job. They might have been given this house, but they couldn't stay here without more money.

Chapter Six

Grant

Grant glanced up from his paperwork as the front door to his office jingled. He grinned as Nick's stepson walked through the door.

"Jack! Haven't seen you here in a while. What's up?"

Jack shrugged. "Not much. It's career exploration day at school. I'm here to work with Dad."

Grant shuffled through some paperwork and pulled out a rumpled copy of his schedule. "That's right, Nick was telling me about it. He's already on the job site. I'm headed there in ten minutes. If you can wait, I'll drive you."

Jack nodded and sat down in the armchairs they used for customers. "Thanks. I can wait."

Grant finished placing his supply order online and glanced over at Jack. The boy was scrolling through his phone, nodding like there was a soundtrack in his head that only he could hear. As he watched, Jack started tapping his feet and hands to the beat.

Grant grinned. To be fifteen again. At that age, he'd been chasing girls all over town, trying to work up the nerve to ask out Avery—the one girl who mattered to him. Not that his nerves stopped him from dating lots of other girls.

Nick was going to have his hands full.

His best friend had met Jessica shortly after high school. She'd been a single mom at that point, raising Jack on her own after having him at sixteen. Grant looked at the boy again out of the corner of his eye. Man, he couldn't imagine raising a child at Jack's age. At the same time, he thought for sure that he would have kids of his own by thirty—and here he was, alone. We make plans, and God laughs. Wasn't that how the saying went?

Grant pushed himself away from the desk and stood up. He moved toward the office door, gesturing for Jack to come with him. "Thanks for waiting. I didn't see you at trick-or-treat last night. What were you up to? You're not getting too old for candy, are you?"

Jack grinned and pulled a lollipop out of his pocket. "Nah, my sisters did all the hard work. They shared their candy haul. I didn't feel like dressing up, so I went down to the beach to build a sandcastle."

"Who else was there; Liam, Chloe?"

"They had to help their brothers go trick-or-treating, but it was fine. Some little girl showed up and asked if she could help. She was dressed like a princess. We won best princess castle."

Grant had seen a lot of princesses last night. Only one stuck out in his mind, though. He wondered if Avery had listened to him and made her way to the beach. She'd always loved watching the sandcastle competition. "Glad you had help. Did you know the kid?"

"I've never seen her before. Her name was Sophia. Her mom helped a little, too."

Grant grinned at the thought of Avery making a sandcastle with Jack. Nick's stepson was one lucky guy.

When Grant parked his truck, Nick waved the boy into the house and walked over to greet Grant.

"I hear your girlfriend was busy last night."

Grant rolled his eyes. "I don't have a girlfriend. Not enough time, remember?"

Nick leaned against the truck and crossed his arms. "You've got time. You'll have a girlfriend soon, too."

"With you in charge? I'll be married by next week." Grant shook his head, knowing that he just needed to put up with the ribbing.

"You're coming around. I'm proud of you, man. So anyway, I heard that Avery's daughter was building sandcastles with my son. If you dated her mom, our kids could spend more time together."

Grant reached in for his toolbox and pulled it out of the truck bed. "That's the angle you're playing this time? Poor Jack, he needs a friend?"

"Whatever works. Come on, let's talk seriously for a minute. Step into my office," Nick said. He held open the door to Grant's truck.

"That's my truck."

"I helped you pick it out, so I'm claiming it as my office today. Besides, I've got three kids. I do my best thinking in a truck, alone. Work with me."

Grant sighed and climbed into the truck. It seemed like Nick would be taking his match-making advice to the next level this time.

Once the two of them were settled, Nick turned to face his friend. He frowned and furrowed his forehead in concentration. "This is going to be weird, but trust me. Okay? Close your eyes."

"How weird is this going to be?"

"Just close your eyes."

"We've got a house to put back together," Grant said, sighing even louder. Still, he knew that arguing with Nick would waste more time, so he closed his eyes.

"Okay, imagine yourself in high school. You're young. You're happy. I have more hair."

"Very funny. Okay, we're in high school again."

"You've got a science project due tomorrow. I'm working, so I can't help you. Who do you call?"

Grant didn't hesitate. He'd always asked Avery for help in school. Nick was a good friend, but she got the best grades. "I'd call Avery."

"She was great in science class, wasn't she? Now imagine prom night. We're not all going as friends this time. You've got to pick one girl. Who do you pick?"

Grant thought for a moment, but it wasn't a hard question. "Avery. Brook hated school dances, but Avery always had fun."

"Fair enough. Now imagine yourself in the future. You're sixty years old and retired."

"That's not going to happen."

"We've got big plans. You'll be happily retired by then," Nick said. "Close your eyes. You're walking along the beach at sunrise. There's a woman by your side, holding your hand." He paused, giving his friend a moment to imagine the scene. "Don't overthink it. Just imagine it. *Whose hand are you holding?*"

"Avery." Grant's eyes flew open. "I'm holding Avery's hand. And that makes me happy. How did you do that?"

Nick shrugged, looking smug. "The best matches don't happen by pushing together two random people. If you want to build a happy couple, you need two people with things in common. You and Avery were always friends. Maybe you can be something more."

Grant stared at his friend, trying to untangle his thoughts. "On some level, I think I've always wanted that. But Avery just wants to be friends. What should I do?"

Nick reached for the door handle and shrugged. "Be her friend. If that's what she needs right now, give it to her. Most women know what they want. Be her friend, and then make her want more. You just need to give her time."

Grant threw himself back into the truck seat. "That's your advice? Give her time and make her want more. How do I do that? We're going out for coffee in a few hours."

"We'll discuss that at next week's session. For now, go have coffee with a beautiful woman. Good luck."

Chapter Seven

Avery

The door's bell rang cheerfully as Avery stepped into Seaside Cupcakes.

She took a deep breath and looked around. Tables with whimsical centerpieces were clustered in one corner. A display of coffee mugs sat on top of a display case; the case was filled to bursting with fresh cupcakes, muffins, and cookies.

And the smell? It was wonderful. Avery hadn't slept well the night before, and the aroma of coffee and sweets brought out a tired smile. She wasn't just here for coffee, though. She was on a mission.

She was meeting Grant here in about fifteen minutes. Before he got here, she needed to clear the air with her friend, Brook. The two of them had been so close in high school; but just like she'd left Grant, she'd left Brook behind without looking back. Brook deserved a better friend.

Today, Avery was here to be that friend. She marched to the counter and rang the service bell.

"Just a minute," a familiar voice called. "Let me get these cupcakes out of the oven."

Avery drummed her hand on her thigh, determined not to be pacing when her former best friend saw her for the first time.

Brook burst through the door separating the shop from her kitchen. "Hello! How can I help... Avery. Is that you?"

She threw her towel onto the counter and rushed around the display case. She wrapped her arms around Avery in a hearty hug. "I heard you were back in town," she said, giving her friend one last squeeze before holding her at arm's length to look at her. "How long are you staying? If I didn't hear from you in a few days, I was going to track you down. I've missed you so much!"

Avery stared at her friend, dizzy from the whirlwind welcome. She'd been ready to beg for forgiveness, and her friend had accepted her with no questions asked. Grant had been the same way. She didn't deserve friends like Grant and Brook.

She smiled and squeezed her friend's hands. "I'm back, and we plan to stay. But look at you! Look at this bakery. How are you doing?"

"I'm great. Pull up a chair." The two of them sat next to a table facing the front window. "Are you meeting someone else, or did you stop by to say 'hi'?"

Avery blushed. As often as she told herself that she was just looking for friendship, today's coffee meet-up felt like a date. "I'm meeting Grant for coffee soon. He should be here any minute."

"That's my girl. You're lucky Grant is still available. Grab him while you can, because that man has aged like a fine wine." Brook nodded as if she had been studying Grant for years, waiting for the right time to pluck him off the shelf.

Avery burst out laughing. She'd forgotten how much fun Brook could be. "No, no. We're just friends. I'm not ready for a rebound. I'm not ready to bring a man into my daughter's life, either. Even someone like Grant."

Brook leaned forward and put her hand on her friend's arm. "I heard about your ex-husband. I never met him, but your grandfather didn't like him much. You're better off without him."

Avery nodded and stared out the window, avoiding her friend's eyes. "You should have met him. You might not have liked him, but we were best friends. You should have met him."

"Don't start that," Brook warned her. "I made mistakes too. I should have reached out after you left, but I was too busy. Do you remember the catering business we worked for in high school?"

Avery nodded again. Of course she remembered. They'd spent every Friday night, and almost all day Saturdays, working in this building to prep and serve food. Back then, the building had belonged to Seaside Catering. Together, they'd helped the small community celebrate almost every wedding, funeral, and anniversary in town.

"After high school, I picked up more jobs. I lived at home and saved every penny I earned. After a few years, I was a head baker at Seaside! I bought the building when the owner decided to retire, and kept part of the business name. It's not much. But it's all mine."

Avery looked around in amazement, noticing the changes Brook had made. "It's a huge accomplishment. I'm proud of you. You knew what you wanted and you went for it. All I've got to show for the last ten years are divorce papers that my husband won't sign, and a lawyer that keeps calling me. The only positive thing I've made since high school is Sophia." Avery's voice warmed as she thought about her daughter, and she held up her hands in surrender as Brook gave her a knowing look. "Okay, okay. I've made at least one good thing. But there are days I wish I hadn't settled into being a wife and mom and nothing else. I had bigger dreams."

Brook reached in and gave her friend another hug. "We're still young. There's lots of time to live your dreams! Plus, if Sophia is anything like her mom, I'm sure she's great. I can't wait to meet her. Bring her in for cupcakes soon."

Avery gave her friend a quick squeeze. "I will. It's so good to see you."

The women turned as the front door opened and Grant walked in.

Brook stood up and marched toward their friend. She poked a finger into his chest and scowled. "You've known Avery was home for days, and you didn't bring her into my shop until today. Not acceptable."

Grant grinned sheepishly and shoved his hands into his pockets. "She's here now. I thought meeting here would be a good idea."

Brook threw her hands in the air and sighed. "Yes, yes. You're forgiven. But don't let it happen again. I'll let the two of you get settled. What would you like?"

He slid into the seat vacated by Brook and considered his options. "One double-chocolate muffin and a large black coffee, please. Avery, what do you want? It's my treat."

Avery didn't love the idea of letting him pay, but her empty bank account demanded more attention than her pride. She skimmed over the menu and pointed. "You make sticky buns! Did you keep the old recipe from Seaside Catering?"

"I did. What do you want with your sticky bun?"

"Iced coffee with vanilla cream, please."

Brook grinned as she sashayed back behind the display case. "You've still got your sweet tooth. I love it! Be right back with your order."

True to her word, Brook was back with two coffees and the rest of their order before the friends even had time to build an awkward silence.

Grant sighed as he sipped his coffee and set the cup down. "Brook makes the best coffee in town. They're almost as good as her cupcakes. Try your coffee—she makes her own whipped cream."

Avery's eyes widened as she tasted her own drink. It was sweet, with a deep, creamy flavor that she hadn't expected. Brook had always been talented in the kitchen. She hadn't been satisfied to just work for a caterer; Brook wanted to make her own creations. She'd spent most summer days experimenting in the Brown family kitchen and perfecting recipes.

She lifted the cup for another sip, but was interrupted by her phone. "Sorry, it's my lawyer again. Let me send this to voicemail."

"Are you sure you don't need to answer it?"

Avery rolled her eyes and shrugged. "He's been updating me on the divorce. It's not going smoothly. My husband promised to make this easy, but he's argued about almost every point. I just want full custody of Sophia and a clean break."

Grant frowned and nodded. "That seems reasonable. I'm sorry he's making this so hard."

"I'm not surprised. He makes everything difficult." Avery's eyes widened and she slapped her hand over her mouth. "Sorry. I try not to talk bad about him. He's Sophia's dad. I'm ready to be done with him. I just wish he wasn't hurting our kid in the process."

"She seems like a good kid."

"She's the best. I'm so proud of how well she's holding up. She jumped right into school. The teachers say she's doing great."

"Of course she's doing great. Look at her mom. She's got a strong support system."

Avery blushed again. "I'm doing my best. Do you have any kids?"

Grant laughed and took another swig of coffee. "No kids yet. I'd like them eventually, but I haven't met the right woman. I've been so busy at work that I haven't had time to look around, though." He stared at her long enough to make her blush deepen. If she hadn't known better, she'd think he was looking at *her* in that way.

Avery looked down at her fingers and fiddled with her high school class ring. She didn't want to see Grant's warm, green eyes staring at her. She'd made a lot of mistakes, and she was starting to think leaving Sunset Cove was one of her biggest mistakes.

Grant seemed to sense her discomfort. After a few seconds, he cleared his throat and took a big bite of his chocolate muffin.

"Now that you're back, you can try all of Brook's desserts. She's a genius in the kitchen." He seemed anxious to fill the silence and spoke around the mouthful of food. Finally he swallowed, took a gulp of coffee, and grinned. "Her cream-filled donuts are the best. They sell out every morning. They're worth getting here early."

"Don't flatter me!" Brook called from behind the counter, where she was ringing up another customer. "I'm not saving donuts for you."

Avery and Grant glanced at their friend and both burst out laughing.

"She hasn't changed much, has she?" Avery asked.

Grant finished the last bite of his muffin, then wiped his mouth and crumpled the napkin into a ball. "She hasn't. She's still spunky and spicy, and the most loyal friend you could ask for."

"Have the two of you…"

"Dated? Eloped? Got together for weekly donut-eating competitions?" Grant's eyes twinkled with humor. "No, never. We've never been more than friends. I wouldn't say no to more donuts, though."

Avery picked up his napkin and tossed it at his chest. "You're such a guy."

Grant grabbed the napkin in mid-air and leaned forward. "Is that a problem?"

She blushed again, but didn't break eye contact this time. "You've been my best friend since elementary school. No, it's not a problem that you're a guy."

"Excellent." He reached across the table and started to gather their trash. "I've got to get back to work. Nick will have a field day if I'm not there to keep him in line. But this was fun."

"It was fun. It was wonderful to catch up."

Grant threw their trash away, then dropped a bill in the tip jar and waved goodbye to Brook. The two of them were silent as they made their way toward the door. He seemed nervous, Avery noted.

"Maybe… If you want to… Could we do this again?" Grant asked, stopping and turning to face Avery.

"You want to come back for coffee again?"

"No. I mean, sure. I'm up for coffee any time," he said, his brow furrowing as he struggled to find the right words. "What I'm trying to say is, let's not be strangers. I want to spend more time with you. And Sophia seems like a lot of fun. If it's okay with you, I'd like to get to know her."

Avery hesitated. She'd just promised herself that she wouldn't bring a man home for a long, long time. It was too confusing for Sophia.

But Grant wasn't a random guy, was he? They weren't dating. They were just friends. Sophia might understand that her mom could have both girl and boy friends.

"You're too quiet," he said, making a face that she remembered as his 'I've messed up' look. "If you don't want to get together, that's fine. I'm sure we'll run into each other around town."

"No, it's fine," she said, digging through her purse for her cell phone. "Put your number in my phone. I'd love to get together again soon. It's been too long! I'm sure we can find something fun for the three of us to do."

She chewed on her lip as he tapped in his own number. His phone pinged a second later.

"Done. I texted myself. Now we have each other's numbers," he said, checking his phone. "Things are slowing down for the fall, but we can find something for all of us to do. There's always something happening in Sunset Cove."

Avery smiled and put her phone away. "I remember. Fall was my favorite season."

Grant checked the time, then backed up a few steps. "I'm sorry, I've got to go. See you soon?"

"Yes, see you soon! Thanks again," Avery called, watching him walk out of the bakery.

To her surprise, she felt a pang of loneliness as the door shut behind him. What was that about? They were just friends. Close friends with years of history, but still just friends. She'd been living without her childhood friends for a long time.

That was the problem, she realized. It had been years since she'd had a real friend to talk to. Lately, all of her friendships were superficial—connecting during a school fundraiser, or business dinners with other couples. She didn't have a chance to build deep relationships. Even Eric had become distant over the past few years.

Avery would need to be careful. It wouldn't take much to jump from friendship into love.

Chapter Eight

Avery

Avery started to follow Grant out the door. She stopped when Brook called her name.

"The two of you are cute together. You always were." Brook had a wide smile as she stepped out from behind the counter.

Avery shook her head adamantly. "We were never together. Not in high school, and not now. We're just friends."

Brook slid onto one of the barstools lining the counter and patted the seat next to her. "Sure, you're just friends. But when you're ready, I think he's willing to be more."

Avery rolled her eyes and hopped on her own barstool. It felt natural to sit next to her friend, like no time at all had passed. "Since when are you a matchmaker? Nick is the one who builds couples. You're too busy breaking every boy's heart."

Brook tipped her head back and laughed. "I don't have time to break hearts anymore. I'm too busy building my bakery. But we're not talking about me. We're talking about you and Grant."

Avery swiveled her chair to face her friend and considered her next words. "Grant seems like a great guy. He always was."

"Yep. Go on. Explain why you're still just friends."

"First of all, I'm married. On paper, anyway. Our divorce should be final soon. But until that happens, I'm still Mrs. Avery Brown-Goodwin."

"Details. You've signed the papers, right? You're just waiting for some judge to make it official."

Avery cut her off, hopping off her stool. "I'm waiting for Eric to sign the papers, too. I'm not ready. Sophia's not ready. We need to get our lives together. Find a job. Start building a home here, because Grandpa's house is a mess."

Brook sighed and stepped down from her stool, then put her hands on her friend's shoulders. "You will get your lives together. And I have a feeling Grant will help you every step of the way. As a friend, or as something more. I'm guessing that choice will be up to you."

She spun Avery toward the wall. There was a "We're hiring" sign next to the cash register. "I can help with part of your problem, though! Can you still frost cupcakes and mix cookie dough? I'd like to expand, but there aren't enough hours in the day to do everything."

A job in the bakery? Avery knew she needed to find work soon, but hadn't thought about working with food again. Their catering days felt like a lifetime ago. She had a college degree in business management—not that it had helped much while she was a stay-at-home mom.

"I don't know. It's been a long time since I worked in the kitchen..."

"Please say yes! I'm flexible. You can work around Sophia's school hours. Heck, bring her here on days off." Her friend spoke quietly, pleading. "I miss you. We should work together again."

Avery searched her friend's face, worried that this might be a pity offer. But Brook didn't look sorry for her. She seemed excited at the idea of hiring her.

"Are you sure? It sounds like fun. I'm a hard worker, but I'll need some time to relearn everything."

"Yes, I'm sure! Let's do this. Can you start tomorrow?" Brook asked, going behind the counter and searching through the drawers. "I just had new shirts made." She tossed a light blue shirt toward Avery and grinned. "You could start tomorrow after you drop Sophia off at school."

Avery smiled back. Brook's excitement was contagious. She was already looking forward to getting back into baking. She'd cooked almost every night as a stay-at-home mom, but her favorite memories from the city were teaching Sophia how to make cakes, cookies, and pies. Now she'd have a chance to bake every day, and maybe even bring Sophia into work. Her daughter would like that.

Brook reached for Avery's hand and tugged her behind the counter. "Let me give you a quick tour. It's not much, but I've got plans to update the kitchen and seating areas. Grant said he would help. He just hadn't had enough workers to get everything done."

She pulled Avery into the kitchen. The setup hadn't changed much since their high school days. There were still two industrial stovetops and ovens. Brook had managed to squeeze in a few more cooling racks. She'd also swapped out the racks of pots and pans for muffin and cupcake tins.

"I've done the best that I can with the space. I need more ovens if I'm going to ramp up production. I haven't used the stovetop as much as we did for catering." She sighed and leaned against the counter. "It's time to make some decisions. I either need to start offering a lunchtime menu or commit to expanding the bakery. Either way, I need you. I can't keep doing this alone."

Avery nodded, looking around the space. "I can't believe you did this all by yourself. There were ten of us working at Seaside Catering! Thank you for hiring me. I'll work hard and do my best."

Brook waved her hand. "I'm not worried about that. You're a hard worker and I can't wait to spend more time with you. But I do need the help. It was tough keeping up this summer. Tourist season is winding down, so it's a good time to jump in and learn the ropes."

She led her friend out of the kitchen and past the display case. "I'll need to do something out here, too. More room for tables and chairs. Some hardscaping out front and outdoor seating. But it's too soon to think about all of that. Let's take it one day at a time! I'll see you tomorrow after you take Sophia to school?"

"Sounds good. Thank you again. I'm grateful for the opportunity."

Brook gave her friend another hug. "Thank *you*. We're going to be a great team. I've been looking for the right person to hire for a while now."

It was funny how life worked out. Avery had come to Sunset Cove thinking she was out of options. Maybe the divorce and move had been a blessing in disguise.

Just then, her phone pinged. She shifted her new work shirt to her other hand and checked the message. "It's Grant. He wants to take Sophia and me to the lighthouse festival. That was fast."

Brook danced around behind the counter and clapped her hands. "Of course it was fast! He couldn't risk waiting too long. Another guy could snap you up."

"It's not a date. We're just friends."

Brook wiggled her eyebrows. "Sure, you're friends right now. But is that all you want?"

Avery shook her head. It was just like being back in high school. But that's what happens when you move into a small town, she thought. For better or worse, everyone knew everything about you.

But at least small-town friends had your back, even when times were tough. She'd been completely alone as her marriage fell apart in the city. Things might have been different if she'd had some close-knit friends.

She waved goodbye, promising to return at eight a.m. for her first shift.

On the walk home, she thought about all that had happened in the last hour. She'd regained two friends and found a job. It had been an amazing day.

She stopped at the mailbox outside her house and pulled out a stack of envelopes. The post office had stopped forwarding the house's mail to her brother, and she was shocked by how much mail there was each day. Starting over caused a lot of paperwork. Avery sorted through the letters as she opened the front door and walked into the house. There was a letter from the school welcoming Sophia to the area; an advertisement from the grocery store; and an envelope from the Sunset County Tax Office.

Hmmm. That seemed important. She started to rip open the envelope but was interrupted by the front door flying open.

"Mom! I'm home! I had a great day!"

Avery set the envelope aside, eager to tell Sophia about her new job and their plans to visit the lighthouse festival. The mail could wait. Her family would always come first.

Chapter Nine

Grant

Grant opened the door to the O'Neill house to see Nick standing by the front door.

"So, how did it go?"

"Good, I think. We talked and caught up. I got a little nervous at the end, but I texted her a few minutes ago. We're going to the lighthouse festival this weekend. Her daughter's coming with us."

Grant closed the door behind him, eager to get back to work and burn off some nervous energy. He was still surprised that he'd worked up the nerve to ask Avery and Sophia out for the night. It felt like just yesterday he'd been too chicken to ask her out. But they weren't in high school anymore. It was time to man up and show Avery that they were meant to be together. Even if that meant being friends for now.

He still wasn't convinced that Nick's plan would work. But Nick was the one who was happily married, so he would take all the advice he could get.

"The lighthouse festival is a good start," said Nick. "You've got to spend more time with her. Remind her how much fun the two of you had together. Show her what life would be like if you were together all the time."

Grant shook his head. Nick's confidence amazed him. "Are you sure this is going to work? Shouldn't I just ask her out on a date?"

"Nope. If you move too fast, you'll scare her away. Trust me. When I wanted to date. Jessica, I started slow. She wasn't ready to date either. All you can do is give her space and wait for her to be ready."

He picked up his safety glasses and slid them in place. "Besides, you do want to be friends, right? What's the worst that could happen? You don't get married, but you stay friends."

He gave Grant a wry look and picked up his sledgehammer.

Grant picked up his own hammer. Together, they knocked down the last wall marked for demolition. Once this wall was down, they could start to rebuild.

Grant let his mind wander as they worked. He always did his best thinking on the job. There was nothing like swinging hammers, loud noise, and big messes to help clear your mind.

Would he be happy staying friends with Avery? A week ago, he would have said yes. He hadn't seen his friend in years and was thrilled to have her back in his life. Something was different now, though. Nick had planted a bug in his brain. Each day he thought about Avery a bit more.

He wondered what she was doing.

He wondered how Sophia was doing in school.

He found himself looking for them at the grocery store, the library, and even the school playground. He'd even looped past the school to see if Sophia was outside after their coffee meet-up. Today's non-date had just made the itch worse.

No, he wouldn't be happy being friends. He wanted more.

Once the wall was knocked out and the two men had dragged most of the debris to the curb, Grant pulled off his safety glasses and nodded to Nick. "I don't want to just be friends with Avery. What do I need to do?"

Nick grinned. "I knew you'd come around. I've already told you what to do. Spend time with her. She's just gotten out of a bad marriage. Show her that you're nothing like her ex-husband. Show her that you're reliable and exactly what she needs."

"How do I do that?"

Grant had spent the last few years building his business. There hadn't been much time for dating before now. Sure, he'd taken a woman or two out for dinner. Nothing had moved past the first date. He realized that when it mattered most, his dating skills were badly atrophied.

"She's got a kid. Don't suggest any bars or late nights," he said looking thoughtful. "Try to mix things up. Do a few things with her and her daughter, but don't forget to spend time alone with her. You're working too much. Take time off work and take her to lunch, or surprise her with flowers." He clapped Grant on the back and reached into their cooler for a bottle of water. He handed a second bottle to Grant. "You're a good man, and she knows it. She just needs a little time and space."

Grant nodded, cracking open the bottle. "I can do that. I'll take a few longer lunch breaks this month. Take her out for lunch or a walk on the beach. She loved looking for shells at low tide."

"There you go." Nick seemed thoughtful as he drained the bottle of water. "I had one more idea. It's corny, but hear me out."

Grant groaned. Nick had become the king of domesticated life over the past few years. If Nick thought something was corny, it was bound to be bad.

"My church is looking for people to serve on a new Kindness Committee. Nothing too crazy. They just need people to help around the community and give people a boost. You like helping people, right? Get involved and invite Avery to come along. You'd get to spend time together and show her what kind of guy you are."

Grant put down the bottle of water and stared at his friend. He didn't give his friend enough credit. The guy was smart. "That's a great idea. Do you think Avery would want to help me?" Grant pulled out his phone and opened its texting app.

"Whoa. Easy there. You're not texting Avery already, are you?" Nick put his hand on Grant's phone. "Slow down. You don't want to text her too many times in one day."

Nick pulled out his own phone and began tapping out a message. "Let me give your number to Pastor Rick. He can text you the information about the new Kindness Committee. Wait a day or two, and then you can ask her to come to the next meeting."

Grant sighed and slid his phone into his pocket. "Wasn't it easier in high school? You saw a girl, you liked her, you asked her out."

"Sure, it was easier. Life gets more complicated. If you'd asked Avery out in high school, she would have smiled and gone on the date. You might have kissed her. But now? She's got a little girl to think about. She probably thinks about her husband a lot, too."

Grant frowned. What did Nick mean? Did he think that Avery missed her husband? It sounded like she was lucky to be rid of him.

"Don't worry, she doesn't think nice thoughts about him," Nick amended. "But whenever she thinks about men, she's going to think about the last man she was with. What kind of man was he? He lied, and he cheated. More importantly, he hurt Sophia. Avery isn't going to risk her daughter being hurt again so easily."

Nick picked up a broom and began sweeping the last of their mess. "Life's a lot more complicated since we left high school. But it's also a lot more rewarding. Spend time with Avery. Be a solid friend. That's what she needs right now."

Chapter Ten

Avery

Avery glanced around the kitchen at Seaside Cupcakes. They'd made quite a mess that morning, but it had been a blast. Now there were ten dozen cookies cooling and ready for the deep freezer. In addition to Brook's day-to-day baking, they were preparing for the lighthouse festival.

She hadn't realized the festival was such a big deal. It hadn't been much when she was a kid; just an open house at the lighthouse with a reenactment at the top of the beacon. Brook said that the festival drew dozens of vendors and over a thousand people each year now. She needed to bake dozens of pies and hundreds of cupcakes and cookies to have enough inventory. They'd need to work fast this week and freeze everything so that it would be fresh for the weekend.

Avery wiped up the last of the stray flour and smiled when Brook walked into the kitchen.

"How are you doing?" Brook asked. "It's been a while since you baked on this scale. As you can see, I'm a little overwhelmed. I'm grateful for the help."

Avery grinned. She hadn't baked more than three dozen cookies at a time since she left the catering business. "It was a little crazy this morning, but it was fun. If it's okay with you, I can bring Sophia in tomorrow morning and get an earlier start."

Brook walked over to the giant whiteboard that listed their daily schedule. "We're baking Sunset Cupcakes tomorrow. I need about two hundred of them. If Sophia wants to set out cupcake wrappers, she's welcome to come. She might have fun."

Avery hadn't realized she was holding her breath, but now she let out a small sigh of relief. Eric had treated Sophia like a nuisance. She was too loud, too energetic. She was always in the way, making his own life harder. He hadn't treated his wife much better.

Avery was grateful that Brook embraced her daughter. It was a nice change. "She loves baking. I'll make sure she doesn't cause any trouble. Thank you for being so understanding."

Brook cocked her head and seemed surprised. "Of course I understand. We got into enough trouble when we were kids, but it was a lot of fun. We still got the job done."

Avery giggled and thought about the jokes they'd played on each other in high school. Brook was right. As long as they cleaned up their mess and got their work done, their boss hadn't minded.

"Besides, you're my hardest worker. And you're one of my best friends. Why wouldn't I be understanding?"

"First of all, I'm your only worker," Avery said, laughing. Her grin slowly fell off of her face. "I'm glad you still think of me as one of your best friends. I wasn't a great friend after high school, but that's going to change now."

"I know it is, sweetheart. Now, clean yourself up and come out front. I've got some people you need to meet."

· ♥ · ♥ · ♥ · ♥ · ♥ ·

When Avery walked out of the kitchen, she was surprised to see four women waiting for her. Three of them sat at the table she'd shared with Grant on her non-date. Brook was busy gathering drinks and donuts behind the counter.

"Let me help." Avery picked up the tray and carried the drinks out to the group. Her friend followed and set a pile of donuts down on the table.

"Thanks," Brook said, sliding into the booth and patting the chair next to her. "Have a seat! These are some of my closest friends in Sunset Cove. Girls, this is Avery! She was my best friend in high school. She just moved back home."

Avery gulped and tried to smile. It came out more like a grimace. She wasn't good with new people. They'd want to know more about her, and then she'd have to talk about Eric and her failed marriage.

Still, Brook *was* her best friend. Right now, she was her only friend. It would be nice to know a few more people in town. She took a deep breath and felt her face relax into a more natural smile. "Hi, everyone! It's nice to meet you."

The woman sitting directly across from her leaned across the table, letting long, blond curls fall across her shoulder. She radiated confidence and warmth. "I'm Kerry Thompson! Welcome back to Sunset Cove," she said, holding out her hand and giving Avery a firm handshake. "I can help with all of your banking needs."

Brook burst out laughing. "Subtle, Kerry. She works at the local bank in the loan department. She helped me open this business, and she's probably written half of the new loans in town. We became friends after meeting many, *many* times to discuss my business plan."

Kerry picked up a donut and grinned. "Who wouldn't want to be friends with the local baker? It's worth it for the free pastries. They were the real reason it took so long to approve your loan."

56

The woman sitting next to her swatted Kerry's arm. "Don't believe that. Kerry has a heart of gold, even if she can eat more donuts than the average linebacker. I'm Rachel, by the way. It's nice to meet you."

Avery accepted Rachel's handshake and examined the petite woman more closely. "I think we've met. Do I know you from somewhere?"

"I'm Ms. Lancaster, the music teacher at Sunset Elementary," Rachel said. "Your daughter just started school, right? I'm outside the school every morning when you drop her off. I can only stay for a few minutes before my lunch break is over, but wanted to stop by and say 'hello.'"

"She didn't want to miss the donuts, either," Kerry mumbled, her mouth filled with chocolate frosting and sprinkles. The rest of the women laughed as Brook handed Kerry a napkin and motioned to the mess on her face.

"Ignore her; she'll be more civil once the food is gone. I also wanted you to meet Emma Miller," Brook said, gesturing to the youngest person at the table. "The two of you should get together. I think your daughters would like each other."

"They're already friends," Emma said, smiling shyly. "It's Sophia, right? My daughter Kendra has been talking non-stop about the new girl in school. They're in the same class."

Avery nodded, amazed again at how quickly friendships formed in a small town. She had spent almost ten years in the city, first building connections as Eric's wife and later trying to make friends with the PTO moms. None of her attempts worked. Every woman was too busy caring for her husband and home.

Even Sophia's friendships had seemed superficial and forced. Their weekends and summers had been filled with scheduled playdates and carefully coordinated school gatherings.

"We'll need to get our girls together," she agreed, delighted to help Sophia form stronger bonds in their new town.

Rachel glanced at her watch and waved her hand to get everyone's attention. "I have ten more minutes. Let's wrap up our thoughts on Thanksgiving before I leave."

Brook turned to Avery and grinned. "You'll like this. Please note that every woman at this table is single. No husbands, no boyfriends."

"Unfortunately, yes," said Kerry. She reached for another donut. "We are all still single."

Brook cleared her throat. "Right. We're single women, a few single moms. None of us have family in the area. We're thinking about having Thanksgiving together. Instead of being alone, we'll make our own family! What do you think?"

Avery looked at her friend, surprised. "I'm just the new girl. You don't need my approval."

Rachel leaned in closer and squeezed Avery's hand. "We're not asking for your permission, honey. We want to know what you think. None of us have cooked a Thanksgiving meal before, and Brook says you used to be in charge of meals like this. Do you think we can pull it off?"

Avery thought back to the Thanksgiving dinners with her grandfather. They were small gatherings, just a few neighbors and her brother. Her grandfather baked the turkey. She made pies and filling. But when Avery compared those meals to the quiet, formal holiday dinners she'd had with Eric, there was no question which was better.

Tears threatened as she thought about this Thanksgiving. It would be her first holiday alone with Sophia. Now these amazing women were creating a make-shift family, ensuring that no one was alone for the holidays.

"I think… that family is who we decide to be close to. And food is just food. If we all took one or two jobs and shared our favorite dishes, it wouldn't be a lot of work for any one person."

"That sounds like an excellent plan," Brook said. "Should we vote? All in favor of a friends' Thanksgiving, raise your hands."

The five women raised their hands. Brook started clapping.

"Fantastic! Wait, we need a toast to make it official." She scrambled to the counter to grab her own drink. "Let's toast to friends who are closer than family. We have a lot to be thankful for."

The women clinked their coffee mugs together.

"Cheers and all that. Now that Thanksgiving is settled, I've got to go," said Rachel. She pointed sternly at Avery. "We've voted, we've done a toast. There's no backing out now! I'll see you at the dinner table."

Avery's eyes grew wide, making Rachel laugh. "Sorry about that. That's the teacher's voice coming out. But you *are* coming to Thanksgiving."

Brook's friends left one by one, offering hugs and a promise to get together soon to plan their upcoming meal. Emma left her phone number and some good days for a playdate.

When the bell over the shop door rang for the last time, Brook walked to the door and locked it with a quick flick of her wrist.

"Phew! What a day." She walked back to the office and brought out a notebook. "Before I forget, this is my receipts book. I keep all of my records here. It's got a place for time sheets too, see? Log your hours here. I trust you, but I want to make sure I'm paying you for all the hours you work. I'm giving you a key, too. You can come in as early as you want on festival weeks."

Brook held out a small silver key. Avery took it and thanked her friend, touched that she trusted her again so quickly.

"I don't want to be rude, but we haven't talked about my paycheck yet. How often will I get paid?" Avery asked, thinking about the bills that were starting to pile up on her kitchen counter. They hadn't brought much from Eric's house, and she had put some school clothes and groceries on a credit card. She hadn't worked up the nerve to open the tax bill yet.

The next few months would be difficult. At least she knew that the holiday would be cheerful, thanks to her new friends.

"You'll get paid every week. I'll give you the first check next Monday, for this week. Is that okay?"

"That's perfect."

"Great. Let's get cleaned up and pull those last pies out of the oven. The timer should go off any minute." Brook began wiping down the counters and motioned for Avery to stack their dishes in the sink. "What did you think about today?"

"About the job, or your friends?"

"Both."

Avery grinned. She hadn't been with a group of rowdy, friendly women in a long time. Her last group of enthusiastic friends might have been in high school. Brook was the leader back then, too. Her friend's enthusiasm for people always amazed her. She had a real gift for bringing people together.

The job had been fun, too. The two of them had worked hard, but they'd worked side by side. Measuring ingredients, mixing dough, scooping, pouring, and baking. Brook had been in and out of the kitchen while the shop was open for customers, which had given Avery some quiet time, too.

"They were both great," she said. "I'd forgotten how much I love making food for others. And your friends seem amazing. I hope they liked me."

"Don't worry. They loved you," Brook said. "How could they not? I still think this will be your last Thanksgiving as a single woman, though."

Avery threw her oven mitts at her friend. Of course she would still be single in a year. She wasn't even divorced yet, and she needed to be careful for her daughter's sake. Grant was just a friend.

Chapter Eleven

Grant

Grant paced nervously in front of Avery's house. He'd texted her a few days ago, inviting her to join him at the Kindness Committee meeting. Sophia was spending the afternoon with Emma and her daughter.

It was strange being back at the Brown house. He'd spent lots of time here as a kid, eating meals with Avery, her brother, and her grandfather. He'd done most of his high school homework assignments sprawled on a couch in her living room. They'd even taken their group prom pictures in front of these hedges.

The hedges were overgrown now. He should offer to help her. It was tough taking care of a house and a child by yourself.

While he'd been here many times, today felt different. They weren't supervised by her brother and grandfather anymore. They weren't children anymore. Avery had a little girl of her own.

His friend reinforced that thought as she opened the door and came down the front steps, smiling. She wore a knee-length dress with some sort of wrapping sweater on the top. It was something she would have worn in high school when she wanted to make a good impression. But she wore it differently now. Her body had softened and filled out through the last decade.

No, she wasn't a child anymore.

"I'm ready," she said, unaware that her simple outfit was making Grant's knees weak. "You left your truck at home. Are we walking to the church?"

"We are, if that's okay. It's not far."

"That's true. I've spent too much time in the city. You couldn't walk anywhere from our condo." She wrinkled her nose. "Eric had a driver take us most places. There was so much traffic that I didn't want to drive."

Grant tried to imagine that. Living in a small town had given him a sense of independence from a young age. Before he could drive, he'd biked everywhere or walked. He'd bought his first truck as a teenager. He couldn't imagine depending on someone else to get around. She'd lived a very different life since they left high school.

"Do you miss living in the city? There must have been a lot to do."

"There was a lot to do. The quiet is nice here, though." She walked silently for a minute, then took a deep breath and held out her hands. "The city never smelled like this. It's so fresh and clean. And I can hear the ocean from here! I hadn't realized how much I missed the slower pace."

Things did move slower here. Grant wasn't going to argue with that. But as he looked at the pretty woman walking next to him, he wondered how slowly he'd have to move to convince her to be more than friends. He looped his arm through hers like they'd done in high school, hoping to remind her of what she'd left behind.

"It's a great little town," he agreed. "It's settled, then. You missed the town, so you can never leave again." He smiled playfully as Avery grinned back.

"That sounds like a plan."

·♥· ♥ ·♥· ♥ ·♥·

Grant and Avery walked through the back door of Grace Lutheran Church and headed toward the conference room. They knew where they were going. While neither had been inside the building in years, they'd both attended Sunday School in this church.

"Do you still come here on Sundays?" Avery asked.

"I've gotten out of the habit. Nick comes every week with his family, though."

"Maybe I'll come with him one week. See what the new pastor is like. He moved to Sunset Cove before my grandfather died. Grandpa liked him."

They walked into the conference room and saw a tall man with a clerical collar talking to the gathered group. Avery nodded toward him and lowered her voice. "We might get a chance to meet the new pastor right now."

As if he'd heard her comment, the pastor turned to the two of them and smiled. "Hello! Pick a seat. We're about to get started. We have a lot to cover in the next hour."

Grant and Avery pulled out chairs near the back of the room and sat down at the conference table. Grant greeted a few people, then noticed that Avery didn't seem to recognize anyone. He reminded himself to take a few minutes for introductions. He guessed it was tough being the new person in town.

Scratch that. She wasn't new, but she might as well be. The town had grown a lot since she left. That couldn't be easy.

The tall man cleared his throat and clapped his hands twice, then walked to the front of the room. "It is wonderful to see so many of you here. Welcome! I'm Pastor Rick Harris. I'm the head pastor at Grace Lutheran. I recognize a few of you, but I don't know everyone in the room. Why don't we take a few minutes to go around and introduce ourselves?"

As each person gave their name and their ties to the community, Grant saw Avery sink into her chair. He'd forgotten that she didn't like speaking in front of crowds.

When it was their turn, he introduced himself as the owner of Grant Construction and a friend of Nick Butler. Then he turned to Avery and smiled. "This is my friend Avery. I'll let her introduce herself."

She pulled back her shoulders, seeming to steel herself against her nerves. "I'm Avery Brown. I grew up in Sunset Cove, but just moved back after a few years of living in Philadelphia. I moved into my grandfather's house on Ocean Drive."

One of the older men leaned forward. "Are you Clint Brown's granddaughter?"

"I am. I lived with him until I graduated from high school."

He nodded eagerly. "I thought you looked familiar! Name's Harry Anderson. Your grandfather was a good man. He helped a lot of people in this town." He extended his hand across the table. "Welcome back. It's good to see you again."

Grant watched as Avery tentatively shook the man's hand. She blinked rapidly. Oh, no. It looked like she was going to cry. He really couldn't handle it when women cried. He put his arm around her and gave her a quick squeeze. "Welcome back," he whispered.

She smiled at him and leaned into the hug, then turned her head to focus on the next person introducing himself.

When everyone was done, Pastor Rick reached for a stack of papers and began handing them out. "Now that we all know each other, it's time to start brainstorming ideas. One individual can't do a lot. Sure, each of us could work alone and donate a few dollars or a few hours of our time. But if we work together, we can move mountains."

"What kind of mountains do you want to move?" Harry asked.

The pastor nodded. "A mountain can be almost anything. There are children who can't afford to buy lunch at school. The school has a program set up to sponsor those kids, but they're always low on money. We could hold a fundraiser for them."

He walked around the room, speaking more quickly as his excitement grew. "I've got a neighbor down the street who needs a handicapped ramp built. I'd gladly donate money to pay for the supplies, but I don't know anyone who can build it. When Grant walked into today's meeting, it gave me an idea. Maybe I could ask him to donate an hour or two of his time to build a ramp."

Grant nodded. "I can do that. You make an important point. We've all got something we can share, whether it's money or skills. And once we start helping people, maybe more people will join in."

"Exactly," said Pastor Rick. "When someone needs help, we'll go into our network and find ways to help them. It's a simple idea, but the web of resources that we're going to build will be complex, with lots of strands. The more strands of people and resources we have, the more we can make this town a better place to live."

Grant sat back in his chair, thinking of what the pastor had said. He thought about what Nick had told him, too. He'd been working too hard. Even a month ago, he'd have laughed at the idea of joining a committee like this. There weren't enough hours in the day to work and volunteer, too. Then he looked at Avery. He thought about her and her grandfather. The two of them had always cared about other people. Her grandfather had helped people until the very end, generously sharing his time and money. He'd left big shoes to fill.

Working together on the Kindness Committee could be a start. It was just a bonus that he'd get to spend more time with Avery. She'd loved helping her grandfather as a child, weeding the public gardens and helping to serve hot chocolate at the town's Christmas tree lighting. Hopefully, this committee would help her bring back some of that joy and give her a reason to put down new roots in Sunset Cove.

The group shared a few ideas, and Pastor Rick wrote each of them on a whiteboard at the front of the room. The most promising idea seemed to be a fundraiser. The group would need money to get started. If someone came to them looking for gas money to start a new job, or a few dollars to pay their heating bills, they should have money that they could donate with no questions asked.

Plus, a big fundraiser would spread the word about their work. More people might get involved, volunteering to help and pointing out needs in the community.

Grant watched as Avery slowly raised her hand. "My daughter's school did a Zumbathon last year. It raised a lot of money and my daughter said it was fun. Have you done anything like that around here?"

Harry chuckled and pretended to be confused. "I've never heard of a Zoom in the Amazon. But if the kids like it, that's good. They'll bring their parents. We need to get everyone involved."

Avery laughed, clearly delighted with the old man. "Zumba is like dancing with music, but everyone does the same dance at the same time. A Zumbathon is a dancing marathon. You charge admission. My daughter's school sold snacks and drinks. They even had a basket raffle."

"I like that idea." Pastor Rick wrote it down. "We host Zumba at this church every week. The organizers are passionate about helping the community, so they might be willing to help us. Would you help, too?" he asked Avery. "If we work quickly, we can raise money before the holidays. What do you think?"

When Avery nodded, Grant raised his hand. "I'll help too. Zooming Amazons sounds like fun," he said, grinning at the old man, who cackled and shook his head.

Pastor Rick wrapped up the meeting and asked people to continue thinking of ideas. They agreed to meet again in two weeks to finalize the plans for their first fundraiser.

As people walked out of the room, Pastor Rick stopped Grant and Avery. "Thank you for helping with this first fundraiser. What we do this fall will have a big impact on what kind of program we can run the rest of the year." He turned to Grant. "I was serious about someone needing a handicapped ramp, though. We've got someone at the lumber yard who's willing to donate supplies at cost. Could you build a ramp for one of our church members this weekend?"

Grant nodded. "I'd be happy to. Give me the address. We'll walk by the house to get an idea of how big the project will be, and I can schedule a time with my crew. If it's just a simple ramp, it won't take long."

Once they had the address, Grant realized that the house was between the church and Avery's home. "Let's check it out now. Do you need to be home soon?"

"Sophia's eating dinner with her new friend. I've got time."

The two of them walked toward the address they'd been given by Pastor Rick. The silence stretched between them, but Grant didn't mind. It felt like they were back in high school, content to just walk quietly together. He hadn't realized how much he'd missed her over the past decade.

Avery counted the house numbers out loud, making Grant chuckle. He'd been working on houses in this town for years. He knew exactly where the house was. "We're looking for Mary

Marino's house. It's the blue ranch home with a few steps out front."

They stopped in front of the house and Avery verified the address. It was a small house, with just three steps leading up to the front porch, but Grant knew those three steps could feel like a mountain for someone with medical problems. His mom had struggled with steps at the end. He'd built a similar ramp for her house.

"This shouldn't take long. Just two or three hours if we work together. You're going to help, right?" He turned to her and grinned, then threw his head back and laughed when her eyes widened. "Relax. I won't make you use the circular saw, but you can still help. Keep the site clean, bring us supplies as we run low. Maybe run for lunch if we get hungry?"

He bit back another grin as Avery let out a deep sigh of relief. "I can do all of that. Just let me know when you need help."

"How about Friday afternoon? We've got the lighthouse festival on Saturday, but we should be able to get this done after your bakery shift and before school gets out. I'll pick you up at your house. Just Nick and me. We won't need the other crew members for such a small project."

"It's a date!" She stuttered as she considered the words. "I mean, it's not a date. I'll see you on Friday."

Grant chuckled again. "I will see you for another non-date on Friday."

He grinned from ear to ear as he walked home from Avery's house. They'd had a good time together again, and they'd get to spend two more days together this weekend.

Life had definitely improved since Avery moved back to Sunset Cove.

Chapter Twelve

Avery

Avery's hand shook as she put down the tax bill. There had to be a mistake. According to this bill, she owed $22,410 in overdue taxes and interest. Her family hadn't paid property taxes for two years.

How was that possible? Her grandfather passed away last year, but he was an honest man. He took pride in paying his bills and taking care of his own house. If he was struggling to pay the bills, he would have told her. Wouldn't he?

Besides, any financial problems would show up in her grandfather's estate. Her brother Brad was in charge of the will and everything else. It had been his idea to move here. He would have warned her if they owed money.

She read the letter again, paying careful attention to each word.

> *Please be advised that this is your final warning. All overdue taxes must be paid by money order before Friday, December 1. Tax liens not settled in full by this time will be sold at the county's tax auction on Monday, December 4.*

She called Brad but hung up when the call went to voicemail. At this point, she wasn't sure what type of message she might leave. Brad had mentioned their grandfather didn't leave a lot of money in his estate, but she'd never imagined there were overdue bills.

Her thoughts flickered to Eric. She quickly shoved that idea away. Sure, he could pay off this bill without blinking. Thousands of dollars was a drop in the bucket for him. But he had already warned her not to ask for alimony, and the amount of child support she was asking for was laughable.

Besides, she was ready to put her ex-husband in the past. She'd solve this problem on her own.

She leaned over the table and rested her head on her arms, using the dark, quiet space to think. Yes, she would do this without Eric. Besides, she wasn't entirely alone. She slid her phone back out of her pocket and texted her brother.

> *I need to talk to you.*
> *Call me as soon as possible.*

She put down the phone and took a deep breath.

They would figure this out. Hopefully, this was a mistake. Just a mix-up in the paperwork. They would laugh about it later. Even if it wasn't a mistake, she would find the money. The bank couldn't sell the house with less than a month's notice. She would find a second job and pay the taxes over time.

Her gaze lingered on the fridge, where she'd hung Sophia's newest painting. Her daughter had come home with the artwork after her first day of school. She'd been so excited that day.

Avery had to figure this out. There would be no other second chances.

She rushed to gather her tax paperwork, along with the credit card bill forwarded from her old address. It wasn't a big bill compared to the property taxes, but it was one more thing to pay off.

Avery closed her eyes, forcing herself to stop pacing around the room and think. What should she do first? She needed more money, yes. But she would need a place to deposit her paycheck next week and write checks for her bills. She needed to go to the bank. First, she would open a checking account. Then she could ask if she qualified for any loans against her income or the house.

She grabbed a piece of paper and scribbled out a list. One step at a time. She hadn't survived Eric's betrayal to let one bill knock her down, even if it was the largest bill she'd ever received.

By the time Grant and Nick arrived a few minutes later, she wore jeans and a hoodie, ready to work. She pushed aside any thoughts of money and pasted a smile on her face. She had played the role of a happy wife for years, faking it at every social event and parent-teacher conference. Today, she would master the role of a carefree, happy friend.

"Let's do this! If I do a good job today, you can let me use the circle saw."

"It's a circular saw," he said, looping his arm through hers. "Let's start small. Have you ever used a hammer before?"

· ♥ · ♥ · ♥ · ♥ · ♥ ·

Avery had never used a hammer before.

She had other skills, though. Avery cleaned up wood scraps and helped Nick carry lumber from their trailer to the front of the house.

She had even packed a basket filled with snacks and sandwiches. Hungry children were unproductive children, and Avery suspected men were the same way. So she kept their bellies full, and the coffee flowing, as the two men stayed hard at work.

"Is that a turkey club sandwich?" Nick asked, tossing his gloves to the ground. He tore into the sandwich, ripping off a big bite.

"Jessica doesn't keep lunch meat in the house," Grant explained. "She says preservatives aren't healthy."

"It's the listeria. Her OB told her to avoid lunch meat while she was pregnant. Now she's afraid we're all going to die from listeria," Nick mumbled, spewing bread crumbs as he spoke. He wiped his mouth. "Sorry. This is delicious."

Avery grinned, glad she had made one person's day brighter.

Once the three of them finished their sandwiches, Grant waved her over to the ramp. He handed her a pair of work gloves far too large for her hands.

"Let's get to work. You need bragging rights. Every time you drive by this house, you can tell Sophia you helped build this ramp."

"Is that what you do? Talk about every project you've ever done as you drive around town?"

Grant chuckled. "Sometimes. It depends who's in the truck with me."

"He's not wrong," Nick chimed in. "My kids won't let him in our car anymore. They're tired of hearing the remodeling history of Sunset County."

Grant rolled his eyes, then picked up a hammer and nail. "It's not hard. I'm going to hold the nail. You're going to swing the hammer."

Avery picked up the hammer and held it an inch away from the nail. She gave it a tap and heard the *tink* of metal hitting metal, but the nail didn't budge.

"Try a little harder," he said. "You need more force to push the nail into the wood."

She held the hammer further away, closed one eye, and gave it a harder tap.

"Both eyes open, please." He gently pulled the hammer out of her hand. "Depth perception is important, and you need two eyes for that to happen. Watch me. Hold it above the nail and give it a good whack."

He pounded the hammer into the nail, then gave it two more quick taps. When he moved away to show her the finished result, the nail was flush with the wood.

Avery's eyes widened as she considered her next move. "I'm not good at this. If I swing hard, I'll hit your hand."

"I trust you," he said simply. "Besides, I've hit my hand plenty of times. Keep both eyes open. Eyes on the nail. Follow through."

She hit the nail harder this time and felt a flush of satisfaction as it pushed into the wood. After five smaller hits, she was done.

"I did it," she said, holding out the hammer. "How did I do?"

Grant grinned at her and took back the tool. "You did great. No one can say you stood aside and watched other people work. What do you think? Are you ready to use the circular saw now?"

She glanced at Nick, who was pushing a loud, rotating saw so that it bit through the wood with a high squealing noise. The power tool broke the board into two pieces in just a few seconds.

"I'll stick to hammers, but thanks. The saw is a little intimidating."

The two men measured and trimmed boards, working swiftly while Avery stood on the sidelines. She jumped in when she had the chance to help Grant heft a piece of wood into place.

"I wish I could help more," she said, feeling awkward as she stepped aside and gave Grant room to work. "You're doing most of the work."

"You're not just watching. Don't forget, you hammered in a few nails. You've been helping us carry supplies around, too," he said, nodding to the dwindling pile of boards. "Nick and I work well together, but a third set of hands is useful. It makes the project go more quickly."

Nick nodded and pulled his gloves off, then grabbed another sandwich and a bottle of water. "My wife, Jessica, does the same thing sometimes. She packs food and keeps us on task. It's exactly what we need."

Grant pulled another water bottle out of the cooler. He took a long gulp. "Don't forget what Pastor Rick said about our skills. We all have different talents. When we work together, we can move mountains. This ramp isn't a big project, but it will make a big difference in our neighbor's life. You helped make it happen."

Avery leaned against a trailer, thinking while she watched the men work. Sure, she'd hammered in one nail. She'd made enough food to help them keep working. And she'd carried a few pieces of wood. She couldn't do much else.

It was a depressing thought. She had a job now, but she also had enormous bills to pay. Unless Brad found money hiding in her grandfather's estate, she'd need to think of more ways to raise funds.

What was she good at? She could stretch a dollar. That would be an important skill over the next few months. Eric had plenty of money, but he'd often given such small budgets for parties and holidays that she needed to get creative. She was grateful for those challenges now. Her daughter had food, clothing, and school supplies, without going into too much debt. She had enough debt to deal with already.

What other skills did she have? She thought about the last few years. She was an excellent trophy wife, which wasn't something to brag about.

Avery tried to be a good mom, too. She could draw an excellent stick person and cut just the right amount of crust off a sandwich.

The school PTO had raved over her cookies. They sold out at every bake sale. At least she could use that skill at Brook's bakery, she mused.

The sun was close to setting as they finished the ramp and packed away their tools. The three of them climbed into Grant's truck, then made the short drive back to Avery's house.

Grant hovered outside his truck, holding the door open as he waited for Avery to climb out. "I like working with you. Did you have any fun?"

She stood in front of him, gazing up into his green eyes. "I had fun," she admitted, thinking back to the laughs they'd shared over sandwiches. It reminded her of their younger days, when they'd spend nearly every day together. "I liked being part of the team."

Nick leaned over and started cranking up the truck window. "Don't mind me. I'll give you two a moment."

Grant chuckled as Nick finished closing the window. "It was good to see you again, Avery. I'll pick you up tomorrow?"

Tomorrow was the lighthouse festival, she remembered. Sophia had been looking forward to it all week. They would need to help Brook move baked goods to the site, but then she was free to spend time with Grant and her daughter at the festival.

"Yes, tomorrow still works," she said. "Meet me at the Seaside Cupcakes table. I'll be helping Brook at the table when we're not walking around."

"See you soon," he said, leaning in to give her a quick kiss on the cheek. Avery blushed and waved goodbye as the truck pulled away from the curb. She reached up to brush her cheek. She promised herself she would remain friends with Grant. Her heart wasn't ready for more, and neither was Sophia. Now, with this tax bill hanging over her head, she had more to juggle than ever.

It had been a nice kiss, though. She didn't feel pressured.

She decided to focus on the positive things. Today had been nice. Tomorrow would be another good day.
Worries about the future could wait.

Chapter Thirteen

Grant

Lost in thought, Grant didn't notice his good friend's grin.

Nick stared at him, his eyes shining with glee. The matchmaker looked thrilled. "That was a fun project. I was a little worried, though. Sparks were flying. I didn't want to burn the new ramp."

Grant glanced at his friend, then turned his attention back to the road. "I didn't see any sparks. We're just friends, remember? I'm waiting for her to make the next move."

"That little kiss was a smooth move." Nick continued to grin. He threw his head back and laughed at Grant's confused expression. "You really are clueless. Did you ever kiss Avery in high school, even on the cheek? And did you see the way Avery stared at you while you worked? She wasn't watching me like that."

Grant drummed his fingers on the steering wheel. "She was watching me?" The idea sent a thrill through him. He'd paid attention to her, too. Avery had been cute as a teenager, but she'd matured into a beautiful woman.

She might not know how to use a hammer yet, but what she lacked was confidence. She could figure out a few tools if she had enough time and confidence.

Still, she had been helpful. People underestimated how important it was to have support on the sidelines: a person to help carry bulky boards or pack a quick lunch. They made a good team. It would be nice if she was always by his side.

Surprised by the direction of his thoughts, he jerked his attention back to the road and lurched to a stop at a red light. The two men flew forward into their seatbelts. "Sorry," he mumbled. "The light turned too quick."

He eased onto the gas when the light turned green, but soon found his thoughts drifting back to Avery.

Sure, the day had been fun. He hoped they would start dating, eventually. But how far did he want to go? To his surprise, he imagined her on the O'Neill job site, helping him to do the finishing touches once the project was done. Bringing Sophia to pick out paint samples. The three of them gathered around his tiny kitchen table, laughing and sharing a meal.

Nick cleared his throat, interrupting Grant's daydream. "You missed the turn to my house. I'd offer a penny for your thoughts, but I don't need to. You're thinking about Avery."

Grant sighed. "Why can't I stop thinking about her? She's not even ready to date."

"Not yet. But she will be, one day. You're playing the long game."

Grant narrowed his eyes at the suggestion. "I'm not playing a game. People get hurt when you play games."

Nick threw up his hands in surrender. "Take it easy. I'm friends with both of you, remember? I know you don't want to hurt her. And she's not the type to enjoy games. Just don't forget to think ahead. What will you do when she's ready to date? There are clearly sparks."

Grant couldn't help himself. His face lit up in a grin as he made a U-turn toward Nick's house. "There were a few sparks. I liked it. What do I do now? I'm taking her and Sophia to the Lighthouse Festival tomorrow."

"Keep spending time with her. It sounds like her ex-husband didn't treat her very well. Aunt Jane said he was cheating on her.

He demanded the divorce and kicked Avery and the kid out of his house."

Grant gripped the steering wheel, flexing his hands as a flash of anger burned through him. "Your aunt hears too much gossip."

"She does. She also told the person spreading rumors to keep their mouth shut. Avery doesn't need baggage while she's trying to start over. Anyway, I wanted you to know. She's just ended a terrible relationship. Sounds like she needs a friend right now."

Grant's anger simmered to a low boil. What kind of man cheated on his wife? Avery had been a wonderful person in high school. She deserved a man who would treat her with respect. Someone who would cherish her and Sophia.

Could Grant be that person? The last of his anger drained away, leaving a glimmer of hope.

"What do I do?" he repeated.

"Show Avery how a real man treats a woman, especially one he cares about. Keep spending time with her and Sophia. What are your plans tonight?"

"I don't have any," Grant said, using his turn signal and pulling onto Nick's rural road. The truck bumped over the dirt road. It was a marked contrast to the smooth streets where Grant and Avery both lived. "I was going to order pizza and watch some football reruns."

When he pulled into Nick's driveway, two kids and a large dog came racing toward the truck. Nick grinned as he stretched his arm toward the truck's door handle. "I complain about the noise at home, but miss these guys when I'm gone. Instead of watching football, bring that pizza to Avery's house."

"Are you sure?" Grant pulled out his phone to text Avery, then hesitated. "I don't want to push too hard."

"Text her first. Make sure she doesn't have plans. Women like their alone time, but I'm guessing Avery's lonely tonight. Sophia's spending the night with a friend, right?"

"Yeah. Sophia's having dinner with Emma's daughter. Are you sure she won't mind if I stop by?"

Nick grinned and pushed open the track door. "She didn't mind that kiss, did she?" Jumping out of the truck, he slammed the door and kneeled down to embrace his two youngest children.

Grant watched the happy family for a moment, then unlocked his phone.

> You hungry? I'm getting a pizza with half pepperoni.
>
> It's the perfect pizza for sharing.

He stared at the phone, watching as three little dots danced across his screen while she typed a reply.

> Avery
>
> *You can't eat pizza alone. Should I come to your house?*

Grant grinned. This was easier than he expected. He pulled up their favorite pizza place's app to order the pizza, then typed a reply to Avery.

> Stay home.
> I'll see you in 30 minutes.

Thirty-two minutes later, Grant pulled his truck to the curb. He was proud of how much he'd gotten done in the last half-hour. He grabbed the pizza and some flowers from the grocery store and walked up to ring the doorbell.

With a small smile he held out the flowers, saying, "These are for you. Thanks for the company today, and the help."

Avery blushed deep red and opened the door further to let Grant into the house. "Thank you. They're beautiful. Let me find a vase."

She dug through her grandfather's cabinets, searching for a vase. She found a tall pitcher that would work and filled it partway with water. "I can't believe you're still hungry. I made eight sandwiches and the three of us ate all of them! It's been a long time since I've fed a working man."

He laughed and pulled two plates out of the cabinet, plus a pile of napkins. "If I remember correctly, you and Brook used to help cater the annual work parties. There were lots of hungry workers. I can't imagine how much food they ate."

"It was a lot," she agreed, sliding a slice of pepperoni pizza onto her plate.

Years ago, the town had rallied each summer to finish a project. Once they'd rebuilt a man's garage after a fire. Another year, they'd built the church pavilion. They'd always had the support and guidance of a local construction company.

The projects had stopped a few years ago, as some volunteers grew older and the youngest helpers became busy with their own lives.

Despite the work they accomplished, that wasn't what stuck with him from those days. He clearly remembered standing on a ladder, looking down at Avery as she heaped platters of food on a nearby table.

The scene had struck him senseless. Avery looked just as tasty as the sandwiches they were putting out. He'd been surprised by his reaction. Still, he'd done nothing about it. Those memories had faded over time, but now that Avery was home, those feelings were returning—but stronger.

They carried their plates and blankets out to the porch. It seemed like Avery never missed a chance to be outside now, despite the cold. She claimed to be soaking up the fresh air and ocean breeze.

After spending the day together, the pair didn't have much to talk about. They sat together on the porch, not speaking, content to enjoy the food and each other's company. One by one, the stars came into view.

This wouldn't be a bad way to end most days, Grant realized. Maybe Nick was right about having someone to pull you home each night.

Still, he wanted to give Avery some space. They were still just friends. When he saw Emma's car pull up with two little girls chattering in the back seat, he stood up. "It was a good day. Thanks again for the company."

He considered leaning in to give her another kiss, but wasn't sure how she would react in front of Sophia. Instead, he reached down and squeezed her hand. "I hope you like the flowers. I'll pick you up tomorrow."

· ♥ · ♥ · ♥ · ♥ · ♥ ·

The sun was peeking over the horizon when Grant drove his truck toward Seaside Cupcakes.

Brook was taping up a sign that said "Closed for today: Meet us at the lighthouse!" She jumped in surprise when Grant parked in front of her. "What are you doing here? It's six o'clock in the morning. Shouldn't you be building something? Or asleep?"

"Avery said you're moving a ton of food to the festival this morning. I thought you could use some help."

Brook put her hand on her hip and smirked. "That's funny. I've been doing this festival for five years, and you don't offer to help until Avery's involved. I see how it is." She pushed up her sweater sleeves and opened the door for Grant. "I'm a little jealous, but I'll take any help I can get."

"I never realized you did this all yourself," he said, walking into the shop and pushing through the kitchen door. "If you'd said something, I would've helped every year."

He walked into organized chaos. Sophia stacked trays filled with frozen cookies onto the counter. Avery packed boxes with pies, carefully nestling them to not break the thawing shells.

"Grant, Grant, Grant," Sophia chanted. "We're going to the lighthouse today. Did you come to buy a cookie? Brook says they're selling these cookies at the lighthouse."

He chuckled and straightened the tower of cookie boxes Sophia had assembled. "We're going to the lighthouse together. Will you climb to the top with me today? The view is beautiful from the top of the lighthouse."

"Yes!" She turned to her mom. "Can I? I'm good at climbing steps."

Avery tucked a stray hair into her braid, making Grant's heart stutter. How did the woman manage to look so beautiful this early in the morning?

Fortunately, Avery remained oblivious to his inner turmoil. She paused her work to face her daughter and friend. "We can climb the lighthouse if we have time. Let's focus on getting these boxes and trays into the van right now. Grant, why are you here?"

"I thought Brook could use a hand," he said, stumbling over his words. "Didn't want to show up for the fun if there was work to do, too."

Brook barked out a laugh and pushed the first trays of cookies into his arms. "We'll keep you busy. Bring these trays to the van. We'll stack them on the racks. The boxes filled with pies can go right on the floor."

The morning passed by in a blur. The four of them packed the van and tucked a few extra pies into Grant's truck. Then they drove to the lighthouse, Grant following the van into the already-crowded park.

Taking in the lively scene, he marveled at the crowds of people enjoying crafts, food, and music in the park. He hadn't been to the festival in years.

Grant hadn't expected the park to be this busy, and was glad he had offered to help. Brook and Avery shouldn't handle this crowd on their own.

They spent the next few hours helping Brook sell treats to hundreds of hungry people, each eager to enjoy a slice of New Jersey baking. Sophia joined in, handing out free lollipops.

As Avery sold the last pie to an older couple from Pennsylvania, Brook walked over to Grant and spoke quietly. "I'm going to lock the money into my van. Things are slowing down. Why don't you take your girls up the lighthouse when I get back?"

Grant watched Brook walk away, surprised his friend had noticed his growing affection for Avery and Sophia. They weren't "his" girls, not yet. But he hoped they would be soon.

"Who wants to climb the lighthouse?" he asked, pointing at Sophia. "Do you think you can handle it? It's almost two hundred steps."

The six-year-old wrinkled her nose, not impressed. "I climb at least four hundred steps at school every day," she said. "This should be a piece of cake."

"I like cake. Let's see how you do," he replied.

When Brook came back from the van and gave him a thumbs up, he pulled Avery away from the almost-empty table.

"Come on. She won't miss us for a few minutes. Sophia will want to spend time at the top of the lighthouse, and it closes soon. The view is the best part."

Avery wrapped her arms around herself and gazed up toward the beacon. "I remember. It's crazy, isn't it? Like you're on top of the world, and you've left all your worries on the ground."

"It's a *great* feeling. You've had a rough year. Let's go up and check out the top of the world."

He paid for three admission tickets and they began the slow, steady climb up dozens of steps. Avery called to her daughter a few times, reminding her to stay with them and not march ahead.

"She's got so much energy," she said, stopping to catch her breath on a landing near the top. "I'd love to borrow a bit of her energy. And look at you! You're not even winded."

Grant shrugged and lingered at the window, admiring the view while he gave Avery a moment to recuperate. It was nothing worth bragging about. He was in good shape from his construction job, but he also climbed the lighthouse often. It was one perk of living near the ocean.

His favorite climbs happened at night. Nothing beat looking out at the darkness, seeing only the occasional streetlight and a sky filled with stars.

Sophia started tugging his hand. "I can see the door at the top! We're almost there!"

Grant grinned at her, then turned to check on Avery. "She's right. Can you make it? Your daughter won't wait much longer."

He held out his hand to help Avery onto the next step. She gamely followed him up the last of the spiraling staircase.

When they reached the top, Sophia let out a gasp. "This is amazing! Look at how tiny the people are. I see a boat. And Brook's van. Mom, can we stay up here forever?" she asked, dashing from one side of the observation deck to the other.

"I'm glad we waited until it wasn't busy. Let her have some fun," Grant said. "We've got a few minutes until they kick us out." He winked at Avery, then grabbed her hand and pulled her around to admire the ocean.

"I missed the ocean," she admitted, staring at the waves. "I always feel so small when I'm near the water. But in a good way, like none of my problems are a big deal."

Grant nodded and wrapped his arm around Avery. "I thought my problems in the past were huge. Looking back, they didn't matter in the long run. My mom's health, struggling to start a business... It worked out. Sure, I had to stay in Sunset Cove for my mom. But it helped me create my business here, where I had the support of the entire town. She raised me and I could return the love when she got sick."

And it kept me in this tiny town, where it was easy for us to find each other once you moved back, he thought, picturing his literal run-in with Avery at the grocery store.

After a few more minutes at the top of the lighthouse, an announcement came over the loudspeaker that it was time to leave. The trio climbed down the spiral steps and met Brook at her table.

"What a day. I sold the last of the cupcakes and cookies. We are officially out of food," she said. "I could use help moving these boxes to the van and unloading them at the shop. Do you have time?"

The four of them worked together, helping Brook pack the van one last time. Brook snagged Sophia in a hug and carried her to the front seat. "Sophia gets shotgun! The two of you can drive back in Grant's truck. See you in a few minutes."

She winked at her friends, then helped Sophia with her booster seat and climbed into the driver's seat.

"Alone again," Avery said. "You'd think Brook was up to something."

Grant grinned and opened the truck door for her, then gave her a boost into the seat. "Maybe she is up to something, but I won't complain. I'll never complain about a few minutes alone with a beautiful woman."

"Grant..."

"You're not ready to start dating. But I've had a lot of fun with you, and I want to be more than friends," he said, staring into her eyes and praying that she felt the same way. Enough with the subtlety, he thought. "When you're ready for this to be real, let me know."

"I can't yet," she whispered, shaking her head. A single tear rolled down her face. She wiped it away and smiled. "I can't yet, but I'll let you know when I'm ready."

"You're worth the wait."

Chapter Fourteen

Avery

Avery paced from one side of her kitchen to the other.

She was ready to move on with her life. The first step was to call her lawyer. She'd been avoiding him for weeks. After finishing her shift at the bakery, she had finally returned his calls.

Her lawyer didn't have good news. While she'd hoped he would say the divorce was settled and the papers were signed, he wanted to discuss her grandfather's house instead.

Avery and her brother had hired her grandfather's lawyer to settle his estate. She'd turned to the same lawyer for her divorce. Choosing an attorney so far from Philadelphia might have seemed odd. But he'd been willing to take on the case, and she liked knowing her grandfather's friend was working for her.

Attorney Daniel Rawler was honest but firm. He contacted her husband's attorney regularly, demanding to finalize the divorce.

They'd need to meet again soon. He'd received the overdue tax bill as well, and was calling to discuss the details. "I don't know what happened, but the tax office confirmed the situation. You and your brother owe back taxes on the house," Dan explained.

"Are you sure there wasn't a mistake? Why didn't we get a bill last year?"

She heard the shuffle of papers before he responded. "Last year's taxes should have gone to your brother. They did not. I'd recommend going to the tax office as soon as possible."

"I will. What about money in the estate? What options do we have?"

Dan paused. "Your grandfather and I were friends for a long time. I wish I could fix this. Unfortunately, there's not enough in the estate to pay the taxes. Can you afford to pay the bill on your own?"

Avery let out a bitter laugh. "I'm a single mom, working for the first time in years. I don't have thousands of dollars set aside for an emergency like this."

"I was afraid of that. If you don't have the money set aside, selling the house might be the only way to cover the taxes."

Avery glanced around the kitchen, taking in the worn table, chairs, and retro flooring. The linoleum was faded from sunlight and years of footsteps. She'd done her share of pacing over the past week, but the floor's wear had happened over decades. It was a reminder of how many memories lived in the old house.

Then her eyes fell on Grant's flowers. They stood tall in the vase, looking like no time had passed. But so much had changed over the last few days. She was falling for Grant, despite her determination to guard her heart. And now, she wasn't sure she could afford to stay in Sunset Cove.

"So either way, I lose the house. Is that what you're telling me?" she asked, her voice wobbling with emotion. "We either sell it or lose it to the tax office."

Dan's voice softened as he confirmed her worst fears. "I wish I had better news. Yes, you'll probably lose the house. There might not be enough time to sell, but it might be worth trying. You could use the profit to buy a smaller house in Sunset County."

"What about a payment plan?"

"I specialize in family law, not the tax code. It's up to the county to decide if they'll accept a payment plan. It sounds like they'll want full payment by the end of this month. I'd have a backup plan in place. Unless you're willing to consider…"

Avery held her breath. She would consider almost anything if it meant a stable home for Sophia.

Dan cleared his throat. "I've told you this before. You're entitled to alimony from your husband. If we were able to finalize the divorce with a small lump sum, you could start a clean slate. No tax bill. No need to move."

Avery wasn't sure if she should laugh or cry. Eric was already dragging his feet. She'd given him everything he demanded. She hadn't asked for money, just sole custody of their daughter. Dan had argued, saying it wasn't a fair agreement.

Avery disagreed. She was getting the best part of their marriage—she was getting Sophia. At the time, she'd thought custody of her daughter was worth more than any dollar amount. She hadn't changed her mind, although losing her grandfather's house because of the divorce was a bitter pill to swallow.

"If I ask for money, can't he drag this out even longer?"

"Yes, he can contest the terms. You would win this fight, though. You're entitled to spousal and child support. A judge would decide what amount is fair."

"But we wouldn't settle by the end of this month."

"It's not likely."

"So it doesn't matter. Even if Eric is forced to pay support, I won't get it in time to pay off the taxes."

That settled it. Avery wouldn't embarrass herself by asking her ex-husband for money. She would talk to her brother and come up with a plan. She had to try. Avery leaned over and sniffed the delicate flowers on her counter. She needed to fix this for Sophia and Grant. She owed it to herself, too. She was determined to hold on to her fresh start as long as possible.

She finished the conversation with Dan and sent another text to her brother, asking him to call her. Then she packed up her purse and headed to the bank.

· ♥ · ♥ · ♥ · ♥ · ♥ ·

The teller at Sunset Loan and Savings looked familiar. Avery guessed the woman had worked here for years. She'd come to this bank as a kid, first with her grandfather and later to deposit her own paychecks in high school.

Avery pushed her nerves aside and offered a tentative smile. "Good afternoon. I'd like to open a checking account. I also need to ask about a loan or line of credit."

"No problem," the teller said brightly, pulling out some papers for Avery to complete. She handed her the paperwork and a pen, gesturing toward a desk in the corner. "Let's get you started with a checking account first. I'll join you in a few minutes."

It didn't take Avery long to fill out the forms. She paused at the address line, then scrawled out her grandfather's address and sent up a prayer that she would be living in his home for a long time.

The teller joined her at the desk, taking the forms and entering the information into her computer. Her eyes lit up as she typed. "You're at the old Brown house?"

Avery tucked her hair behind an ear and tried to smile. It came out more like a grimace. "Yes. Clint Brown was my grandfather."

"Oh, yes! I remember seeing you here as a little girl," the teller said, her eyes crinkling with joy. "Welcome back! I'm glad someone's moved into the house. I was afraid a developer would buy it. That's been happening with a lot of older homes around here."

Avery felt her smile tighten into a grimace. Her gut twisted as she thought of her childhood home going up for auction. The idea of a developer buying it to build a newer beach house made her feel sick. "Yes, we're doing our best to keep the house in the family. I live there with my daughter."

"How wonderful," the teller said, not noticing Avery's discomfort. "This is all sorted. You can start writing checks in two business days. I'll give you sample checks to get you started. And here's some information about your account."

Avery nodded and took the bundle of papers. "Do you know if the tax office takes sample checks? I need to pay off my grandfather's bills. The letter mentioned something about a cashier's check." She hesitated, her bravery waning as she thought about asking to borrow money. Still, the bank might be her only hope in this mess. She swallowed her pride and continued. "I'd also like to ask about a loan."

The teller drummed her hands on the table and considered the question. "I don't often work with the tax office. I think you're right, though. They need a cashier's check. And a loan is more complicated than opening an account. Let's find a manager to straighten this out."

Avery let out a sigh of relief. They would straighten this out, and everything would be fine. She wouldn't need to yank Sophia out of Sunset Cove before her daughter finished settling in.

A few minutes later, Kerry Thompson, Brook's friend from the bakery, walked into the lobby.

"Avery! How are you doing?" Kerry smiled as she held open the door leading to her office. "It's great to see you. Our manager is on her break, but I can help you. Come in."

Kerry gestured for Avery to enter the office first. She closed the door behind them. "I've helped almost every person in this town. I never want you to feel weird about working with me. Everything done here is confidential. I tell all my friends that, even if they're ordering checks. Just to get any weirdness out of the way." She grinned and sat in the swivel chair behind her desk, spinning to face Avery.

Avery laughed and settled into the chair sitting in front of Kerry's desk, letting her friend's cheerfulness boost her own mood for a moment. "I forget what it's like in a small town. Everyone knows everybody's business." Her smile fell. "I appreciate the discretion, because I've inherited a problem."

Kerry nodded and reached for a fresh pad of paper and a pen. "Tell me about it."

Avery pulled out the letter from the tax office and explained the situation.

"Since this is the first bill we've received, I need to request a payment plan," she added, smoothing out the paper as she reminded herself not to cry. Tears wouldn't solve anything. "No one in our family knew there were unpaid bills. We need more time."

Kerry set down her pen and leaned forward to look into her new friend's eyes. "This is not the type of welcome you were expecting, I'm sure. I don't work in the tax office, but from what I understand, they don't accept down payments. You'll need to pay the entire amount."

Avery sucked in a breath and handed her friend the letter. "Maybe some sort of extension?"

Kelly's eyes widened as she saw the amount on the bill. "It says the full amount is due on December first. That's three weeks away. I don't think they'll give you an extension, but you've still got time to figure this out."

"Is there enough time to apply for a loan?"

"Technically, yes. But the bank can't use the house as collateral. You don't own the property until the estate is closed."

"What about a personal loan against my income or car?"

Kelly sighed again and drummed her fingers against her keyboard. "You've just deposited your first paycheck. You need sixty days of steady income before we offer a loan. And we don't use cars as collateral. Give me a day or two to think about this. Come back tomorrow, okay? Go to the front desk and ask for me."

Avery agreed and shook Kerry's hand, then walked out to her car. She slumped over in the driver's seat and rested her head on the steering wheel.

She thought of her grandfather's house, looking a bit shabby from neglect but still standing strong.

She pictured her daughter, rushing to see the ocean for the first time, and racing from room to room in their house, eager to explore her new home.

Then she thought about Grant and Brook. Her friends had been her rock. Grant wanted even more than friendship when she was ready.

She would let everyone down.

After a few moments of self-pity, she straightened and turned the key in the ignition. She put the car in drive and drove home.

No, tears wouldn't solve anything. Besides, Kerry was right. They had time to fix this mess. She wasn't giving up without a fight.

· ♥ · ♥ · ♥ · ♥ · ♥ ·

Her brother called while she was sitting on the front porch, waiting for Sophia's bus. "Sorry I took so long. I got a message from the lawyer today, too. Thought I should call you first."

"It's bad, Brad. It's really bad. Unless you have twenty thousand dollars hiding under your pillow, we're going to lose the house."

"Grandpa's house?"

"Of course, Grandpa's house. It's the only house I've got right now." She sucked in a breath and toned down the sarcasm. "Sorry. It's been a rough day, but it's not your fault." She summarized everything she'd learned so far, including the plan to visit Kerry again tomorrow.

Brad cursed quietly into the phone. "I had no idea. I never saw the property taxes for his house. I should have asked why we weren't getting any bills."

Avery slumped down in her porch chair, trying to get comfortable while they brainstormed. "Well, we've got the bill now. What can we do about it?"

"That's the thing. All of Grandpa's money is tied up in the house. A house near the beach isn't cheap, but as far as savings, stocks, or retirement funds? He didn't leave a lot of cash behind."

Avery jumped out of the chair. She didn't want the neighbors to overhear this conversation. She headed to the kitchen and pulled out a mug for coffee. "What does 'Not a lot' mean?"

She heard Brad flipping through papers. After a moment, he cleared his throat. "As of today, Grandpa has.... Two thousand, five hundred and two dollars left in his estate. We can put that toward the bill."

Avery reached for the kitchen chair, dragged it out, and fell into the seat. The lawyer had mentioned that the money was nearly gone, but she hadn't realized it was so dire.

Brad cleared his throat again. "Let's be positive. Some older people take out mortgages against their house. Once they die, the family has no choice but to sell the house. So this seems huge, and it is. But it could be worse."

Her brother always saw the positive side of things. Avery was a more practical person. It didn't matter if they owed twenty thousand or a hundred thousand dollars—they still didn't have the money. Brad was right, though. It could be worse. They had three weeks to tackle this problem.

They both promised to search for more money. Brad thought he could get a loan. Avery would look at her bank account back in the city. It wouldn't be pretty. Every dollar Eric earned stayed in his name. She hadn't added to her own savings in years.

Maybe Brook would give her extra hours or a paycheck advance. She'd have to ask for a lot and just started working. It wasn't fair to take advantage of her friend's generosity.

Besides, if she spent all of her paycheck on taxes, how would she buy things like food and winter clothing? Sophia didn't even own a winter coat that fit. She'd grown so much since last year.

Avery closed her eyes and let her forehead rest on the cool kitchen table. What could she do?

Sitting with her head down wouldn't solve anything. She sat up, pulled a piece of paper toward her, and began to make a list. There were two columns: ways to find money, and things that needed to be paid for.

At least friendship was free. She was grateful to have her small network of support in Sunset Cove. She prayed she wouldn't need to leave town anytime soon.

Chapter Fifteen

Grant

The local ice cream parlor was busy, filled with locals who wanted a sweet treat. Grant slid into a booth and grinned.

"I've got one banana split with extra sprinkles and whipped cream, and one small peanut butter sundae with hot fudge sauce," he said, pushing the ice cream toward Avery and Sophia.

He was thrilled to make Sophia happy with a little treat. She squealed with delight and picked up her spoon. "I love sprinkles. This looks so yummy!" She paused, her spoon hovering an inch away from the banana split. "Mr. Grant, would you like to share? I can get a second spoon."

He bumped shoulders with the little girl and held up his chocolate ice cream cone. "I've got what I want. You enjoy that split. I hope you like it."

Sophia began shoveling the banana split into her mouth. Grant shook his head, wondering at her appetite. They'd had burgers for dinner before going out for ice cream. He hadn't wanted to ruin her appetite with dessert.

The thought made him smile. He remembered Avery's grandfather doing the same thing. Burgers and ice cream had been a regular treat when they were kids.

He took a few licks of his ice cream cone, then turned to Avery. "You're quiet tonight. Is everything okay? Is something wrong with your ice cream?"

Avery took a tentative bite from the bowl, swirling the fudge into the melting vanilla. "It's been a long week. I've got a lot on my mind."

"I'm a good listener," he offered. "If you ever need to share..."

She scooped some melted ice cream into her spoon and shook her head. "Thanks, I appreciate it. This is family trouble, though. I won't burden you with our problems."

Grant frowned and looked at Sophia, who was still happily lapping up her treat. Her face was covered with whipped cream and sprinkles.

"It's not Sophia, is it?" he asked, keeping his voice down. "Or your ex-husband? We're just friends, but I'm always willing to help."

"It's not Eric, and Sophia's fine. I was hoping for a clean start at Sunset Cove. It's been a bit messier than I expected. Speaking of messy...." She reached over to wipe Sophia's face with a napkin. After satisfying herself that the child's mouth was clean, she went back to playing with her ice cream and offered Grant a small smile. "How was your day?"

He suspected Avery was changing the subject, but let it go. She deserved privacy, and it wasn't his place to demand answers. She'd accepted Grant back into her world, and he hoped to stay there for a long, long time. That was all he needed to know for now.

"We finished the O'Neill's second floor today," Grant said, crunching into his ice cream cone and dabbing his face with a napkin. "We've still got to finish the master bedroom, but I'm moving part of my team to a local restaurant. They're closed until the holiday rush for a small remodeling job, and we're on a tight deadline. They make most of their profit between Thanksgiving and the New Year. It's crazy. I can't imagine surviving or failing based on one month's efforts."

Avery sputtered and began to cough. Concerned that she might be choking, Grant moved to her side of the table and patted her back. He kept his hand there, rubbing her back gently in big circles. "It's okay. Deep breaths. Take it easy."

She reached for her water and took a few pulls from the straw. "Sorry. Ice cream went down the wrong pipe."

Grant grinned and handed her another napkin. "You've got a bit of ice cream on your chin," he said, pointing to his own face. "It went down the wrong pipe, huh? It's been years since I heard someone say that. It was something your grandfather liked to say."

Avery didn't reply. She wiped the ice cream off her face and frowned at the table, a deep furrow taking shape on her forehead.

"He was a good man. I miss seeing him around town," Grant said. "I'm sorry you didn't get to move back here while he was still alive. He would have liked having you and Sophia around."

Sophia looked up from her banana split and grinned. "Grandpa always gave me candy. I'm glad we live in his house now. It's a nice house."

Avery's eyes filled with tears as she replied, "It's a great house. You know I grew up there, right? I hope you get to grow up there, too. Excuse me. I need to use the restroom."

Grant frowned as she choked back a sob, threw her napkin on the table and rushed into the women's bathroom.

"Mommy gets sad sometimes," Sophia said quietly, leaning toward Grant as if she was sharing her deepest secrets. "I hear her crying when I'm in bed. And she makes lists. Lots of them, so she doesn't forget to do anything. Adults must have a lot to do."

Grant felt his frown soften as he looked at the little girl. "Adults do have a lot to do. And I know your mom thinks you are her most important job. She would do anything for you. You know that, right?"

"I know," Sophia said, poking at the last of her banana split. "She'd even move into a house that makes her sad. We didn't have anywhere else to go. But I hope she'll be happy here soon. I'm happy here. I want her to be, too."

"What would make her happy?"

Sophia considered the question, dragging the spoon through her melted ice cream. "She's too alone. I go to school all day. She needs someone to talk to after work. She should spend time at the beach, too. That makes me happy. I wish we could move our house to the sand. I could watch the waves out my bedroom window," she said dreamily, staring out the window as if she could see the ocean from the ice cream parlor.

Just then, Avery walked out of the bathroom. Her eyes were dry but rimmed with red. It was clear she'd been crying.

"Are we done with our ice cream?" Grant asked.

"I'm full," Sophia admitted.

Avery nodded. "I'm done, too. Sorry to rush out like that. It was a delicious end to our day. You've got to stop spoiling us."

"What are friends for?" He wrapped his arms around both girls' shoulders. "I have one more trick up my sleeves. Who wants to take a moonlit walk on the beach?"

Avery frowned. "A short walk. It's cold after the sun sets, and we can't be out too late. It's a school night."

"One short walk on the beach, coming up. I always sleep better when I say 'goodnight' to the ocean," he said, turning to give Sophia a wink. Sophia squeezed his hand and winked back at him.

They piled into his truck and drove a few blocks to the ocean. Instead of parking along the boardwalk, he drove a bit farther down the street.

Avery glanced at Grant, then grinned. "Are we going to…"

"We are. Is that okay?"

"It sounds great. Sophia, tighten your seatbelt. This might get bumpy."

Sophia gripped her seat belt and yanked, making sure it was locked tight. Her eyes widened as Grant drove around the edge of the boardwalk and eased his truck onto the sand.

He turned away from a few tourists on the beach with flashlights, driving until they were out of sight. Then he turned to smile at Sophia. "Cars and trucks aren't allowed in front of the boardwalk. That's the part of the beach where people build sand castles, dig holes, and lay on beach towels. But anyone can drive over here if they have a beach tag." He reached up and flicked the dark blue tag hanging on his rearview mirror. "We used to come here to watch the stars at night."

He climbed out of the truck and opened the door for Avery and Sophia. The little girl scrambled down and raced toward the waves.

"Keep your feet dry! You only have one pair of school shoes," her mom yelled, trying to be heard above the waves. But her daughter didn't splash into the water. Instead, she stood at the edge of the ocean and gazed up at the sky.

Grant slid his hand into Avery's. "I remember seeing the ocean at night for the first time. It still takes my breath away."

She stepped closer to him, snuggling under his arm while keeping their hands linked. "Thank you for bringing me here. I've had a tough week. This is just what I needed."

He leaned in to give Avery another soft kiss on her forehead. "Any time. I'm here for you, day or night."

They both stared out at the crashing waves, lost in thought.

Chapter Sixteen

Avery

"Avery! Avery Brown, is that you? I heard you worked here now."

Avery held back a groan as she pushed through the kitchen door carrying a tray of chocolate muffins.

This was happening more and more often. The news had spread that Clint Brown's granddaughter was back in town, and people were eager to see her. It was nice to see familiar faces, and they had nice things to say about her grandfather. But given everything that she was trying to juggle, the nostalgia trips had become overwhelming.

Avery wished she could hide in the kitchen all day. But that wasn't fair to Brook, who asked her to keep the front display stocked during her shift each day.

So instead of running away, she glued yet another smile on her face. "Yes, I'm back," she said, looking at the customer and trying to remember her name. "I'm living in my grandfather's old house. It's nice to be home."

The woman reached out and gave Avery's arm a squeeze. "You don't remember me. I was your principal at Sunset Elementary."

"Principal McFarland!" Her fake smile thawed into a genuine grin. "Of course I remember you. Are you retired now, or are you still working at the school? My daughter goes to Sunset Elementary now."

"I'll watch for her the next time I volunteer at the school. I'm retired, but I help with the kids. Even retirement can't keep me away from my life's calling."

Avery felt a pang as she thought about her former principal's words. Mrs. McFarland was so dedicated. Even retirement couldn't pull her away from her kids. It was incredible.

She wondered what it was like to find a career you loved. "That's wonderful," Avery said, sliding fresh muffins into the display case. "It's nice to see so many familiar faces again. What can I get you today? Our cookies are especially good." She gave the principal a wink. "My six-year-old helped whip up this batch of icing. I promise she was supervised, though."

Mrs. McFarland threw her head back and laughed. "I'm sure she was. You're a good salesperson. Give me a dozen of the cookies that your daughter helped with and four muffins. I'm meeting with the PTO board this morning to discuss our library's expansion. It's nearly done. It's a shame your grandfather isn't here to see it. He should be helping with the ribbon cutting."

Avery paused as she boxed up the cookies, nesting them so that the icing wouldn't smudge. "Oh? Why would my grandfather be there?"

"Didn't you know? He led one of our biggest library fundraisers. We had a rocky start, but we're having the grand opening next month." She took the box of cookies from Avery and held out her credit card, then waved the card around in excitement. "I have a wonderful idea! You should come to the ribbon cutting. You can stand in your grandfather's place, and your little girl can hold the scissors. We do love to involve the children. What do you think?"

Avery took the credit card and swiped it through the machine. She kept her head down, checking the numbers and entering the sales charge before printing a receipt.

Would she and Sophia be living in Sunset Cove next month, or would they have sold the house? Worse, would the tax office force them out of their home?

It would take a miracle to stop either of those scenarios from happening.

"I'm not sure about that," Avery said, raising her eyes to look at her former principal and handing her a pen to sign the receipt. "We're not the best people for the job. We weren't involved at all. My grandfather deserves all the credit."

"Please think about it. He was a wonderful man, you know. We'd love to have his family at the grand opening." Mrs. McFarland lowered her voice and leaned in to speak to Avery, as if she didn't want the other customers to overhear her. "He did a lot more than lead the fundraiser. When we realized we were short money, he offered a generous donation. Thanks to him, we could buy one hundred books and fill the shelves in the new expansion. I was devastated when we lost him. He was so kind and generous."

Avery wretched her eyes away from her work and stared at Mrs. McFarland. She'd known her grandfather was generous, but how did he afford to make such a large donation? Her head spun with confusion. He hadn't had enough money to pay his taxes or set aside for a rainy day. Had he forgotten about his bills? Or had he cared so much about this town that he'd neglected his own needs?

"Yes, he was a very generous man," Mrs. McFarland said again. She beamed at the young woman. "I heard from Pastor Rick that you're just like him. I'm glad you joined the new Kindness Committee. Clint Brown would be proud."

Avery felt a hitch in her throat. Would he be proud? She was a divorced, single mother who had run back home to find a fresh start.

As much as she missed her grandfather, she was glad he wasn't here to watch her struggle. He'd warned her not to marry Eric.

He'd asked her to come home after she got her business degree. She'd refused, wanting to start her own life in the city, far away from the tiny town of Sunset Cove.

She'd give almost anything to see her grandfather one last time. They'd sit at his old kitchen table, share a cup of coffee, and talk about what was worrying him. She should have called or visited more often. If she had, she might understand why his estate was such a mess.

If she hadn't let Eric control her life, keeping her from her grandfather and hometown, it might not have taken so long to realize that their marriage was over.

Avery frowned, filled with regret as Mrs. McFarland walk out the door.

As the front door closed, Brook burst out of the kitchen. She was carrying a tray of her signature beach-themed cookies. She slid the tray into their display case, closed the lid, and brushed the flour off her hands.

"That's enough cookies for today," she said, turning to grin at her friend. "If you won't mind covering the register for a bit, I'll clean up for the day. Maybe we can both leave on time today."

Brook leaned against the counter and looked at Avery more closely. "Are you okay? You look sad. Or angry. Maybe both."

Avery's lip quivered. Between the tax bill, her grandfather's friends, and Brook's kindness, she was a mess. She needed five minutes alone to process her feelings. But there was nowhere to hide. She couldn't even beg for a bathroom break. Brook knew her too well. Grant did, too. She guessed that was why they'd gone to the beach last night.

Was she okay? Avery took a deep breath and started to nod, then shook her head. There was no sense lying to her best friend. "I'm not okay. We came here for a fresh start, but we've fallen right into a mess. Can you keep a secret?" She waited until Brook nodded. "My grandfather wasn't paying his property taxes."

Brook gasped and pulled Avery back into the kitchen, leading her to the chairs they used to take breaks. "That doesn't sound right. Are you sure?"

"I'm sure. We got a letter from the tax office that says we owe... a lot of money by the end of the month. He didn't pay his taxes the year that he died. We didn't even get a bill last year."

Brook's eyes widened as she listened to her friend's story. "This is bad, Avery. Go to the tax office and straighten this out. Tell your brother to bring a check from the estate. Don't wait."

Avery chuckled nervously. "I'm not sure Brad has a checkbook for the estate. There's almost no money left. Grandpa was living off his pension. Selling the house is our most obvious choice—but we might not have enough time to do that."

"That doesn't make sense," Brook said, frowning while she shook her head. "Your grandfather always donated to charities. He was a very generous man."

Avery looked down at the floor. "I wonder if he was too generous with his money. What if he gave it all away, and didn't leave enough for himself? It's something my grandfather would do. He was always willing to give the shirt off his back."

The friends locked eyes, remembering the time Clint had given Avery his winter coat in a crisis. Her parents had been driving home from a pajama party at the school; their car slid on black ice and struck a tree. Avery had climbed out of the smashed car, cold and terrified. Her parents were both unconscious.

When her grandfather arrived, she had been standing alongside the road wearing nothing but pajamas. Clint had bundled her into his coat and rushed her into his car. She'd huddled in the car with Brad while an ambulance whisked their parents away. It would be too late to save her parents, but her grandfather had saved her in every meaning of the word.

Brook reached under the counter and grabbed a tissue box. She handed the box to her friend and reached over to grab a tissue for herself. She let out a loud honk as she blew her nose. "He was a great guy. I'll be praying that your grandfather didn't get in over his head. I'd lend you the money, but things are pretty tight for me, too. I've got every penny wrapped up in this business."

Avery dabbed at her eyes. "It's fine. We'll figure this out. I'm glad I told someone, though. It's a lot less lonely when someone else knows your story. Kerry knows, too. She was going to explore our loan options and meet with me again today."

Brooke looked thoughtful, then reached over and tugged at Avery's apron strings until they came untied.

"What are you doing? I work for two more hours."

"No, you don't. You're going to the tax office now. You need more information before you see Kerry. I'm still paying you for those last two hours, though. You more than earned the money by helping at the lighthouse festival."

Avery shook her head, her eyes brimming with tears again. "I don't deserve to have such good friends."

"Yes, you do. Now go. I want you living in Sunset Cove for a long, long time. You're not leaving us again."

· ♥ · ♥ · ♥ · ♥ · ♥ ·

Avery looked at the tiny woman sitting behind the door that read "Heather Martin, Sunset County Tax Collector."

She put on her most friendly smile and held out a hand. "Hello, it's nice to meet you! My name is Avery Brown-Goodwin. I'm here to discuss my grandfather's tax bill. His name was Clint Brown."

Heather offered a firm handshake in return. "The Brown family estate? Yes, I'm familiar with it. The house is scheduled for tax sale at the end of this month. Such a shame. It's a beautiful house." She settled down in her chair and gestured for Avery to take a seat. "I'm so glad someone came in to settle this. Are you here to update the paperwork and pay off the bill?"

"Not exactly. I think there's been some sort of mistake. My grandfather was always current on his bills. My brother is in charge of the estate, and hasn't received past-due bills before this month. This bill is marked as a final notice."

Heather nodded and turned to her computer. "Let me pull up the file." She clicked around for a few minutes, then swiveled toward the printer as it began spitting out papers.

"Unfortunately, it's not a mistake. As you can see here, your grandfather paid his taxes in installments. Our files show he passed away after making the first of four installments last year. That leaves the rest of last year's taxes due. And once there is an overdue bill, we roll this year's accounts into an immediate-due bill." She handed the printed papers to Avery, as if that settled the matter. "Will you be paying the entire bill today?"

Avery stared at Heather, dumbfounded. "If I had this much money, I would pay you today. I just moved here. This is the first time we've heard about an overdue tax bill. I was hoping to set up a payment plan."

Heather shook her head, her eyebrows pulled together in concern. "I'm sorry. We don't offer payment plans on overdue accounts. On a positive note, you'll qualify for a payment plan next year, once you pay this bill in full."

Avery closed her eyes and tried to swallow the lump in her throat. A payment plan would be great next year. But how would she find the money to keep her grandfather's house *this* year? "I don't understand. Why wasn't this sent to us sooner?"

"Hmm. Let me look deeper."

Avery tried to remain calm as Heather turned back to the computer. How could this have happened? Her grandfather's estate didn't have much money, but this problem would have been easier to solve last year. One month wasn't enough time.

"Here we go! We did mail the quarterly installment bills and a past-due notice. I sent them to the secondary address on file." Heather turned back to the printer and grabbed a fresh piece of paper. She handed it to Avery. "Our last statement came back as 'Return to Sender.' At that point, we sent it directly to the Brown house, hoping we could reach someone in time."

"Where was the secondary address?"

"It's on the paper. Somewhere in Philadelphia. Does the address sound familiar?"

Avery's blood went cold as she skimmed over the report. Her grandfather had listed her as his secondary contact, using her old Philadelphia address.

The problem was that she rarely saw the mail. Her husband insisted on sorting the mail, paying any bills and only handing over the social engagements. That had been her job for the duration of their marriage—ignore the money, focus on appearances.

Eric had been getting these bills since last year. He hadn't paid them. Then he'd had the nerve to send back the latest bill after destroying their marriage.

Her temper flashed from cold to hot. She was tempted to crumple the paper in her hands, but stopped herself. This was a problem to settle with Eric. It wasn't the tax collector's fault.

She spoke through gritted teeth, determined to maintain her dignity and exit the office as quickly as possible. "I see. This makes sense now. There's nothing we can do?"

If Heather had looked concerned before, now she looked positively alarmed. "Is everything okay? We followed your grandfather's instructions. He said that if he couldn't take care of his bills, we should forward the statements to this address."

Avery backed away toward the door, pulling out her cell phone and attempting to give a friendly smile. "It's fine. I know who to call while we straighten this out."

Avery was fuming as she walked toward her car. She texted her brother Brad on the way, explaining the situation. Then she climbed into her car, slammed the door behind her, and called the one person she'd hoped to avoid forever: Eric.

To her surprise, he answered on the second ring.

"I told you not to contact me."

"My grandfather's house. You got the tax bills."

She heard shuffling in the background as Eric covered the phone with his hand. He murmured a few words to someone in the background. After a few seconds, a door clicked shut on his end of the phone.

"Yeah, I got the bills. I wasn't going to pay the old man's taxes for him."

"He was *dead*, not a deadbeat. And if you weren't willing to pay the taxes, why didn't you at least tell me about them?"

Eric burst out laughing. "You were going to pay the bills? You didn't have a job. You just stayed home all day, baking cupcakes for Sophia's school and keeping our cleaning lady company. No. You would have told *me* to pay the bills."

Avery felt her temper surge again. "If I'd known about the taxes, I would have found a job! I would have talked to my brother and figured out a plan. Now we have thirty days to find the money or we lose the house."

"That's too bad," he said.

Why had she ever married this guy? She was tempted to hang up the phone, because he clearly wasn't eager to help. But one thing stopped her: Sophia. "This is your fault, and you're going to help me. Sophia needs stability. I'm calling the lawyer today and adding twenty thousand dollars to the divorce agreement."

Eric laughed again. "Go ahead. I'll make sure we don't settle before the end of this month. By the time you get the money, it will be too late."

Avery stared at the phone, stunned. Eric had become cruel later in their marriage, but she never thought he would hurt their daughter on purpose. More than he'd already done, anyway.

"What if we..."

"Save it. I'll sign the divorce papers this week. Or you can ask for money, and I'll drag this out as long as possible. I might even ask for partial custody. Your choice." He hung up the phone, ending the argument.

Avery set down her phone and slammed her hands against the steering wheel. She couldn't believe Eric's behavior.

After giving herself a few minutes to calm down, she buckled her seat belt and started the car. She had a home to save.

· ♥ · ♥ · ♥ · ♥ · ♥ ·

Avery flung her purse onto the kitchen counter and stalked around the kitchen. She flung open cabinet doors and grabbed a pot and pan. As angry as she was, she was determined to make Sophia dinner as usual.

She set the pot on the stove, this time taking care not to slam it down. Avery didn't have money to repair her stovetop if it broke. She didn't have money for anything, it seemed. They'd have spaghetti and meatballs again tonight. It was Sophia's favorite food. It was cheap, too. Avery wouldn't say no to cheap comfort food.

She let out a growl and slammed the freezer door shut. They were out of meatballs. Resting against the fridge, she sank to the floor and put her head on her knees.

Her meeting at the bank hadn't gone well. As Kerry had predicted, the bank couldn't offer her a home loan until she paid the tax bill. The best Kerry could do was to offer a credit card with a cash advance option. The interest rates were astronomical, but she'd still signed up for the card. She would fight to the last day to save her grandfather's house, and wouldn't let pride or high interest rates stop her.

The card had a five thousand dollar cash limit. Between her own savings account and her brother's savings, they'd dug up a few thousand more. Almost halfway there.

Brad was also applying for a loan, but he wasn't hopeful. Maybe he'd find a few thousand dollars hiding under his pillow. That's where he used to keep his money, back when they were kids.

Avery laughed and shook her head as she brushed tears off her face. She grabbed her purse and rushed out the door, determined to have supper finished on time. Her daughter would be filled with stories about her fun day. She wanted to be ready.

Avery's stomach churned as she thought about the friends she and Sophia would leave behind if they left Sunset Cove. It wasn't fair.

But as Eric had shown her, life wasn't fair. You might do everything right and still end up alone and broke.

Avery headed to the grocery store. They might be broke, but a five-dollar bag of meatballs would not mean the difference between saving or losing her childhood home. Avery's world might be falling apart, but her daughter would still have a normal night.

Chapter Seventeen

Avery

Avery was walking through the front door when her phone rang. A quick glance told her it was the school calling.

"Hello, is this Mrs. Brown-Goodwin?"

She juggled her phone and keys, closing the door behind her while she tried to place the voice. "This is her."

"I'm Megan Nonweiler. From the school? We met when you enrolled Sophia last month."

Avery smiled as she pictured the older woman with long, gray hair and a warm temperament. Of course, she remembered Mrs. Nonweiler. She had been the school secretary for over thirty years. "Yes, hello. How can I help you?"

"I'm sorry to interrupt your day, but there's been a situation at the school. We'd like you to meet with the principal this afternoon."

Avery glanced down at her outfit. Work had been busy today. Despite wearing an apron, a light dusting of flour covered her clothes. She'd hoped to shower after work. If she couldn't shower, she'd at least need to change.

"I can be there in a few minutes. Will that work? Is everything okay?"

"Sophia is fine. She's not in any danger. However, the principal wants to meet with you."

Avery hung up, frowning. She dashed around the kitchen, grabbing the keys and purse she'd just set down. She dragged a hairbrush through her hair and changed her clothes. Within five minutes, she was driving to the school. She met Mrs. Nonweiler at the front desk.

"Thank you for coming. The principal is waiting for you," she said, leading Avery through the same hallways that she'd once walked as a student.

Avery had spent little time in the principal's office as a student. She'd been a good kid, like Sophia. She'd kept her head down and finished her school work each day. Sophia was cut from the same cloth.

The principal's office hadn't moved from its spot near the library. They had remodeled it over the past few years, though. Handsome carpeting covered the floors, and inspirational posters covered the walls.

A tall man with dark hair rose from his desk to shake her hand. "Good afternoon. I'm Allen Sawyer, the principal at Sunset Cove Elementary. I'm sorry to meet under these circumstances, but it is nice to meet you. Have a seat."

He gestured to the table by his desk, then waited while the two of them got settled. He didn't waste time with small talk. "It's come to our attention that Sophia has been cheating on tests and a few classroom assignments. Is this something she's done before?"

Avery's eyes widened. Cheating? Sophia had earned mostly A's at her old school and worked hard for her good grades. "No, she's never cheated. She's an excellent student. What happened?"

"She seems like a good kid, but I'm concerned that she's having trouble transitioning to her new school." The principal explained that Avery was copying answers from her classmates. It had happened once or twice before. "It wasn't until this week's math test that we realized how bad it was. The teacher noticed that Sophia's work was identical to her classmate's. At that point, Sophia admitted that she'd been copying from her friends for several weeks."

The principal slid copies of both girls' tests across the table. Avery shook her head as she examined the two tests. She recognized Sophia's handwriting, but also knew that this wasn't how her daughter had learned to do addition. "I'll talk to her. What will the school do about this?"

"She's only six. We won't be too tough on her. The desks are farther apart now, and we've moved Sophia away from her old seatmate. However, this is still a serious situation. She will receive detention if it happens again."

"I understand. I will make sure Sophia knows it can't happen again."

The principal nodded, then stood to shake Avery's hand again. "Thank you for your support. Sophia's a good kid. We've got to make sure she stays on the right track. Would you like to drive her home, or should I let her ride the bus?"

"I'll drive her home," Avery said, thinking about how her plans for the afternoon had changed. "It will give us more time to talk."

The principal made a quick phone call to Sophia's teacher. Fifteen minutes later, mom and daughter headed home among a swarm of school buses.

Sophia was quiet on the ride home. Avery didn't mention why she was at the school, but she suspected her daughter knew. They were nearly home when Avery took a detour. She turned left off the main road, steering her car toward the nearest beach entrance.

The little girl frowned out the window, realizing they had taken the wrong road. "Where are we going?"

"I thought we'd go for a walk on the beach. What do you think?"

Sophia hesitated, then shook her head and sunk further into her booster seat. "I don't want to look for shells today."

"We don't need to look for shells. Let's go for a walk."

Avery parked the car by the entrance ramp, then opened Sophia's door and looked at her daughter. She was so young. Avery's own emotions felt like the ocean lately, rolling and crashing against a rocky shore. These changes must be even harder for Sophia.

She held out a hand to her daughter and smiled. "I feel better near the water. Come on."

The two walked hand-in-hand toward the sandy beach. Avery turned left at the high-water mark and started down the shore, taking care to avoid the waves lapping at their feet. They walked in silence.

After a few minutes, Avery squeezed her daughter's hand. "The school called me today. What do you think they told me?"

Sophia shrugged her tiny shoulders. She pulled her hand away and walked toward the water, staring at the waves.

"They told me you cheated on a math test, and that this isn't the first time. Is that true?"

Sophia shrugged again and dug into the sand to pull out a large shell. When Sophia realized it was broken, she threw the shell far out into the water.

Avery sighed. She tried to put herself in her daughter's shoes. As a child, she'd never been eager to admit she was wrong. It wasn't easy as an adult, either. She pulled off her coat, bracing herself against the cool ocean breeze in just a sweater and jeans. She laid the coat out on dry sand and pulled her daughter down to sit next to her.

"You're good at math. Why did you cheat?"

Sophia finally looked at her mom, tears rolling down her face. "I wasn't good enough."

"What do you mean? You had A's and B's at your old school. Those are great grades. You don't need to cheat."

"B's aren't good enough," the girl repeated, jerking her coat sleeve across her face. "Dad said I should get A's. If I do better in school, he might let us come home."

Avery felt a surge of anger toward her soon-to-be ex-husband. How dare he make this amazing girl feel unworthy of his love? Eric was the one who wasn't good enough.

She closed her eyes and listened to the waves crash against the shore. When Avery opened her eyes, she wiped away a few of her own tears. "Your dad didn't ask us to leave because of your grades. You know that, right?"

The girl looked up at her mom, her eyes gleaming with tears. "No. I don't know why we had to leave. I want to go home to Daddy. Can we go home now?"

Oh boy. It had been tough to leave, but Avery had no desire to go back. Of course, her daughter thought differently—she didn't know Eric had cheated on them. She didn't realize her dad had already moved on.

"This is our home now," she said, choosing her words with care. She hated promising Sophia that they would stay in Sunset Cove when things were so uncertain. This whole mess, from his disappointed daughter to their financial problems, was all Eric's fault. But no matter what happened, they would *not* move back to Philadelphia. "Should we go back to Grandpa's house? I thought the beach would be a better place to talk, but we can leave."

Sophia shook her head. "I want to go home. To Dad. I can do better. I promise."

Avery gave her daughter a squeeze and held her against her side while she spoke. "You're doing great. I want you to try your best. You don't have to be perfect. We can't go back to the apartment, though. This is our home now."

"Can Dad come here? Tell him I'm doing great. Maybe he'll want to move here."

Avery held back a laugh. Eric, come to Sunset Cove? The man hadn't stepped foot in her hometown during their entire engagement and marriage. She doubted he would come here now, even to visit his daughter. The lawyer had already told her that Eric planned to terminate his custody rights. "He won't come here. But that's okay. We still have each other."

To her surprise, Sophia yanked away from her mother's arms and started yelling. "It's not fair! We're having a Daddy Donuts Day. He's my daddy, and he needs to be there. Tell him to come."

Avery pursed her lips, letting her daughter pull away and run toward the waves again. Suddenly, it made more sense. Her daughter thought Eric had pushed them away for a reason and was trying to fix it. She'd probably felt like this for a while. Daddy Donuts Day had brought it all to a head.

Avery picked up her coat, brushed the sand off the waterproof cover, and walked toward the shoreline. "When is Daddy Donuts Day?"

"In two days."

"How long have you known?"

"They gave us permission slips the day I started school. I hid it in my room, in case Dad visited us."

Avery reached out again and squeezed her daughter's hand. "Oh, sweetheart. You didn't need to do that. Your dad won't be able to make it, but I can come instead."

Sophia yanked her hand away and crossed her arms. "No! I can't bring my *mom* to Daddy Donut Day. If Dad won't come, I need a new dad."

Despite the seriousness of the conversation, Avery laughed. She couldn't help herself. Find a new dad in two days? She'd be lucky enough to find a date as a single mom, let alone someone willing to become a stepdad.

Grant had expressed interest. He seemed to like Sophia. But it was too soon to date. Once Grant realized what it meant to co-parent an older child who wasn't his own, he could walk away, too. She couldn't risk that. Not while Sophia was so vulnerable.

As usual, her precocious child's mind worked rapidly. She frowned at her mom. "Don't laugh. I need a dad in two days. Will Grant be my dad? He was really nice at the lighthouse."

That wiped the smile off Avery's face. "Honey, we can't find you a new dad in two days. Grant is a nice guy. But he's not your dad."

"Maybe he wants to be. Did you ask him?"

Avery almost swallowed her tongue as she considered *that* conversation. "I didn't, and I can't. It's complicated."

"I promise not to cheat again. You can tell him I get A's and B's. Maybe that's good enough."

Avery closed her eyes again and took a deep breath, cursing Eric and his pursuit of perfection. If she thought he would answer her call again, she'd plan a very loud, angry conversation about how much damage he had done. "Honey, you don't need to be perfect for someone to like you. Maybe one day we'll find someone who wants to be your dad. He'll be a very lucky man. But it won't happen today. And not tomorrow, either."

"Okay, so Grant isn't my dad today. Can I still bring him to Daddy Donuts Day?"

Avery stared out at the waves, considering her options. She didn't want to confuse Sophia, but she also didn't want her daughter to feel left out. It wasn't the girl's fault that Eric had abandoned them. Could Grant become more involved in their lives without risking her daughter's heart?

She wrapped her arm around Sophia and gave her another squeeze. "Grant is not your dad, but he is a good friend. Would you ask him to eat donuts as a *friend*?"

Her daughter considered this for a moment, her little face scrunched up in thought. "I'd like it if Grant was my friend. Let's ask him if he likes donuts. Can I find a shell for him, too? Maybe he likes shells."

Avery shook her head as Sophia skipped along the shoreline. She'd lined her grandfather's windowsills with shells as a child, too. She had become more selective as a teen, but Grant had always humored her as she continued her quest to find the perfect shell. It was their time to walk among the waves and talk about their day.

Looking back made her realize she'd been halfway in love with Grant all those years ago. Coming home had stirred up those feelings. But like before, the timing wasn't right. She was still married, and she'd be risking both her and Sophia's hearts now.

As her daughter squealed and held up a perfect, intact clam shell, Avery wondered what Grant would make of the gift. Would it remind him of their own time spent on the beach? Or would he think nothing of the simple gift?

No matter what he thought, she needed to be careful. She was risking both Sophia's heart and her own.

Chapter Eighteen

Grant

Grant sat near the front of The Cove, drumming his fingers on the restaurant table as he waited for Avery to arrive.

She had called yesterday and asked to meet. He was looking forward to lunch with her. Who wouldn't? It was a beautiful setting with a beautiful woman.

Grant watched the waves and smiled. The Cove had been their favorite place when they were teens. It was crowded with tourists during the summer, but the quiet views in fall and spring were worth waiting for.

He thought back to the burgers and fries he'd shared with Avery, Brook, and Nick at this table. You couldn't beat the view. Waving seagrass and a wide stretch of sand separated the outdoor restaurant from the waves. He couldn't imagine leaving Sunset Cove and all of this behind.

"Sorry I'm late," Avery said, rushing through the empty dining area. She made her way toward the table. "I see you grabbed our usual table. Do you come here often?"

"Sure. The food is still good. The old man who owned it died last year, so things are a little different. His son is in charge now."

Avery frowned as she settled in and tucked her purse under a chair. "That's too bad. I was hoping Henry would be here today. He made the best milkshakes in Sunset Cove."

"He sure did. His son does a good job, though. I ordered milkshakes and burgers for us. I hope you don't mind."

Avery put her hand on her stomach and groaned. "I can't eat like a teenager anymore. But bring it on. I'm sure you'll finish anything I don't eat."

They sat in silence for a few moments, watching the waves crash. The seagrass swayed in the breeze. Finally, Avery cleared her throat and squirmed in her seat. "Thanks for meeting with me. I have a favor to ask."

Grant turned away from the water and gave Avery a smile. "For you? Of course. What do you need?"

Avery grimaced. "It's a big ask. Sophia needs someone for Daddy Donut Day. Would you go with her?"

Was he willing to play stand-in for Sophia's dad? He hesitated for a moment. He didn't want to become more attached to the little girl if this relationship wasn't going anywhere. Still, Sophia was a good kid. She didn't deserve to be left out because her dad wasn't around.

Avery seemed to sense his hesitation. She shook her head. "Never mind. Forget that I asked. It's not fair to ask you to step in for Sophia's dad."

He looked up as their server appeared with thick, creamy chocolate milkshakes and two oversized burgers. She set a basket of french fries between them. Grant thanked the waitress, then passed half of the napkins to Avery.

Oh, what the heck. It couldn't hurt to eat donuts with Avery's daughter. He enjoyed spending time with her. He squirted a generous heap of ketchup onto his plate and held out the container of fries. "It's okay. I like donuts, and I like Sophia, too. I don't want her to get confused, though."

Avery nodded. "I've already told her that if you can go, it's just as friends." Her voice softened as she plucked fries off the pile. "She's been through so much. Can I tell you a secret? She thinks you're going to be her new dad. Be careful not to lead her on."

Grant dropped his burger on the plate and took his time chewing as he considered what to say. He would become Sophia's dad in a heartbeat if that's what it took to win Avery over. He was falling in love with both of them, but had promised Avery that he wouldn't push her. "Any man would be lucky to be Sophia's dad," he said, swallowing his food and watching Avery stare at the table. "You both deserve the best."

Avery shrugged and picked at her own food. "I'll settle for a life that doesn't make Sophia feel like she's done something wrong. She thinks the divorce is her fault."

"That sweet little girl? Why would she think that?"

"Eric was pretty tough on her. He expected her to be perfect: perfect grades, perfect dance recitals, the perfect child. She tried so hard, but he was always criticizing her."

Grant's stomach twisted as he thought about how Eric had treated Sophia. It was a huge contrast to his own childhood. His mom had struggled with her health, and money had been tight. But she'd loved him unconditionally.

He hoped to treat his children the same. Kids should know that they've got an adult supporting them. His own dad had left when his mom got sick. He couldn't handle the stress and walked away.

Grant reached over and squeezed Avery's hand. Whatever concerns he had about protecting his own heart, he needed to set them aside and think about Sophia. "She's a tough kid, and she's got a fantastic mom who loves her. It's going to be okay. So yeah, I'll take her to Daddy Donut Day. I would be honored."

⋅♥⋅♥⋅♥⋅♥⋅♥⋅

Grant was having second thoughts. How could he promise to be this little girl's friend? He was already in love with her and her mom.

The trouble started on the morning of Daddy Donut Day. Sophia had been pacing on the porch when he arrived. She looked up at him with big blue eyes and a wide smile, and handed him a perfect clam shell. The gesture was like a punch to the gut. It threw him back twenty years to when another girl shared her best shells with him.

Avery had always loved the ocean, and he'd always loved that about her. Some people took the sand and waves in their backyards for granted. Not Avery. She had saltwater running in her veins, and he hoped her daughter would feel the same.

Sophia gave her mom a big hug and hopped into Grant's truck, her little legs leaping up into the cab. It made Grant think of all the times Avery had hopped into his old pickup in high school.

Grant helped Sophia adjust the seat belt and slammed the door shut. He turned to Avery. "I'll have her back in two hours."

"Take your time. Have fun."

He reached out to touch the side of her face. Then he considered Sophia, and gave her shoulder an awkward pat and let his arm fall to his side. "There are donuts involved. Of course we'll have fun."

Sophia chatted happily for the entire drive, talking about the friends they might see. "Bree and Abby will be there. I eat lunch with them. We're going to sit together today, too."

Grant nodded, his eyes focused on the road while he listened to her talk. Bree and Abby were Nick's daughters. He hadn't realized the girls were friends. At least he would know one dad in the cafeteria.

He pulled into the school parking lot a few minutes later and grinned. Their timing was perfect. Nick was parked next to an empty spot, and he was just getting out of the car with his girls. Sophia squealed and reached for the door handle when she saw them.

Grant touched Sophia's arm. He didn't need her to get hurt less than ten minutes after leaving the house. "Take it easy. Let me help you out of the truck, okay? You're not used to jumping out."

"You help Mom out of the truck, too. Is it too big for us?"

Grant's face flushed as he pictured the last time he'd helped Avery. He'd only held out a hand to steady her, but wanted to do so much more. He pushed this thought aside and held out his hands for Sophia, then grunted as she jumped into his arms. The kid didn't hold back.

Nick grinned as he stood waiting in the parking lot, holding his girls' hands. "Good morning, young lady. Are you ready for donuts?"

Sophia cheered and reached for Grant's hand, gripping it tightly. He looked at their linked hands in surprise. He'd held hands with Avery once or twice since she came home. It was nice to have that physical connection. He'd never held hands with a child before. He felt himself slipping into protective mode, as if nothing was more important than ensuring that the child holding his hand remained safe. She was his top priority. He liked how that made him feel.

Nick followed his friend's gaze, his eyebrows raised. He said nothing as he let his daughters tug him toward the school. Once they were in the cafeteria, the three girls dashed toward a line forming near the front. Each of them grabbed a plate and hand-picked a donut.

Sophia held out a second plate for Grant. "I'm glad you came. I wish my daddy was here, but you can be my daddy for today."

Grant cleared his throat and took the plate, then bopped her on the head with it. "I'm not your daddy, but I'm glad I came, too."

The five of them found an empty table and dug into their donuts. The girls leaned their heads together for a private conversation, quietly giggling while they chatted. Grant and Nick talked about their plans for work next week.

Grant found it surprisingly easy for them to all be together. He'd been friends with Nick for years, but didn't spend a lot of time with his youngest kids. He glanced over at the girls and smiled when he saw Abby's face covered in sprinkles. Sophia dabbed at her face, removing a big blob of chocolate icing. For a moment, he let himself imagine that Sophia was his real daughter.

"I have to go to the bathroom," Bree announced. She stood up and wiped her hands with a napkin.

Sophia stood up, too. "Come on, Abby. Come with us."

Grant watched the girls walk over to the women's bathroom and close the door behind them. "Kids travel in packs, too? I thought only women did that."

Nick bobbed his head in agreement. "They start young. So... you're daddy today? Are you dating mommy now?"

"No, no. It's not like that. Sophia was upset that her dad wouldn't come. She asked me instead."

Nick picked up his soda and took a swig. "Was her dad invited?"

Grant shrugged. He hadn't thought to ask Avery that question. "As far as I know, Avery's husband wants nothing to do with them."

"That's a shame. Sophia's a great kid. I couldn't imagine walking away from my girls. Or my stepson. I'd never leave my kids."

Grant's heart skipped a beat when Sophia came out of the bathroom with her friends. He understood how Nick felt. He was growing closer to Sophia and her mom every day. But it might not be his choice to stay or leave. It would be Avery's choice. She would decide if he was allowed into their lives.

The thought left him unsettled. Kids complicated things. Grant didn't regret waiting for the right woman to start a family, but he'd face a lot of heartache if things didn't work out with Avery.

They finished their donuts and walked around to the rest of the morning's activities. There was a face-painting station, a photo booth, and a small art gallery filled with students' work.

The girls went through the art gallery, letting out shouts of joy as they found their friends' projects. Sophia hadn't been at school long enough to have something on display. Bree and Abby both found paintings from art class.

Nick praised his daughters for their hard work, earning wide grins from the girls.

"I love your artwork!" Sophia agreed. "We can come back next year to see my painting on the wall, too. Right, Grant? Will you come again?"

Grant thought back to Avery's warning—don't let the girl become too attached. Then he also thought about her ex-husband's reaction to Sophia's hard work. It sounded like the man hadn't praised Sophia very often. "I would love to come back, if it's okay with you and your mom next year. Let's see what happens. I'm sure you're a great artist."

Sophia beamed. "I'm an excellent artist. You'll see! Can we go to the photo booth now?"

Grant allowed himself to be pulled toward the photo booth, shooting Nick a look. "Sure, we can take a photo. Maybe just the three of you?"

Bree shook her head and crossed her arms. "No. We always get a picture with our dads. It wouldn't be Daddy Donut Day without Dad."

His friend just grinned and held open the photo booth curtain for Grant and Sophia. "She's right. Let's get two photos printed out. I'm sure Sophia will want a copy."

Grant nearly groaned. Avery would not be happy. He'd promised not to confuse Sophia. But he allowed Nick's family to cram into the booth with him, then smiled for the camera.

The printed photos surprised him. They all looked so happy together. If he hadn't known better, he'd think they were all part of one big family. The thought made him want to slow down. Stop growing so close to Sophia, and give Avery a chance to accept him before he became more attached.

Looking at the photo, he knew that wasn't possible. This little girl was already part of his world, just like her mom. He prayed Avery would catch up when she was ready.

Chapter Nineteen

Avery

Avery smiled as she shifted her phone from one ear to the other. Despite the problems she was juggling, something good had come from her financial struggles—she spoke to her brother nearly every day.

Today, Brad had an update to share. His local bank had approved him for a small loan, too. He would wire the money to her this weekend. "It's not much, but it's all I can do until I find more work. I've got lots of free time, though. I can visit for Thanksgiving."

"It's better than nothing. And it would be great to see you. I'll save a seat at our singles' Thanksgiving dinner. Let's hope it won't be the last time we're together in this house."

Brad grunted in disagreement. "We'll pay off the taxes. Maybe my boss can find another project for me."

"I doubt it. He never has jobs in November."

Brad worked for a construction company in western Pennsylvania. He worked long hours during the summer and fall, then did odd jobs to survive until spring. His last job for the year had ended this week.

She thought of Grant, who wasn't an employee in a construction company. He owned the business. Grant stayed busy throughout the year, doing indoor work during the winter and fixing any storm damage in the town.

It was one of the big differences between the small seaside town and western Pennsylvania. Grant might not be rich, but he gave his employees a full-time job.

Brad had a lot of free time between Thanksgiving and Easter. That gave her an idea. "Don't leave after Thanksgiving. Why don't you pack a few bags and stay over the winter? Sophia would love to see her favorite uncle. It's been ages since she got to spend time with you."

Brad laughed. "Of course I'm her favorite uncle. I'm her *only* uncle. How long has it been since we got together? A year? Two years?"

Avery did the math in her head, guilt gnawing at her as she added up the months. Eric hadn't encouraged her family to visit. She'd rarely seen her grandfather, and her brother had claimed to be too busy to drive to Philadelphia.

She knew the real reason he'd stayed away. Her brother and husband had butted heads from the start, both wanting different things from her. Brad wanted her to be happy. Eric wanted a trophy wife. A rural, blue-collar brother-in-law didn't play into that image.

What had she been thinking? She should have left Eric years ago, years before he ended their marriage. Fortunately, her brother didn't hold it against her. "It's been way too long," she agreed. "Come. Stay at Grandpa's house. If we find the money to keep it, you'll own half of the house."

They had been brainstorming ways to pay the tax bill for days. They were halfway to their goal. It was a start, but they still needed a lot more money. Despite that, Avery was grateful for her brother's daily calls. They might not save the house. That didn't mean she couldn't save her relationship with Brad.

He was silent for a moment while he considered her offer. "There's nothing holding me here until spring. I don't have a lot of money, but I can help you fix up the place. I'm sure being empty didn't help the old house."

"You're not wrong. Pack your bags. Come for Thanksgiving, and stay for Christmas at least. Even if we need to move, you're welcome to come with us."

"Do you still think you'll need to move?"

Avery thought carefully before she answered him. Deep in her gut, what did she think? She was worried. They needed to find a lot of money in a short time. "I'm not sure. It's like we're balancing a dozen plates, waiting to see which one falls first. We might need help to pick up the pieces."

Brad's voice softened. "You can always count on me. You know that, right? And you've got friends in Sunset Cove."

She sighed and paced across the living room floor. If only life was that simple. "Yes, I've got my friends from high school. It's good to be home, and Brook's been a real lifesaver. I told you she gave me a job. But things are tricky with Grant."

"Of course they're tricky. The man's been in love with you since he was a teenager."

Avery stopped pacing and stared at her phone. "What are you talking about?"

"Grant has been crazy about you for years. Everyone knew…" Brad trailed off, letting awkward silence fill the line. "Except you, I guess. I always thought you should have married Grant instead of Eric."

Avery had to admit she'd thought this a few times, too. She let herself wonder again what life would be like if she'd stayed in Sunset Cove. Or if she'd left for school, but returned after college. There would have been fewer fancy luncheons and private school fundraisers—but also less time alone in a big, empty city apartment.

Now that she was back in Sunset Cove, she had to admit she'd missed the small town and all it offered. She loved being at the bakery and taking Sophia to work on baking days. She walked her daughter to school before heading back to finish the morning shift. She had a lot less money, but a lot less stress.

Everything would change if they lost her grandfather's house. She couldn't afford a house close enough to the bakery to keep her job. If they moved out of Sunset Cove, Sophia would switch schools again. She wouldn't be able to spend time with Grant every day, either.

The happy thoughts about her second chance in Sunset Cove faded.

"It's too late to change the past. I can only make the best of the future," she told her brother. "I married Eric, not Grant. We had a child together. If things go too far with Grant and we have to leave, Sophia could get hurt. She's already growing too attached to him. She took him to Daddy Donuts Day."

Avery told him how excited Sophia had been. The little girl hadn't stopped talking about the fun they'd had with Nick and his daughters, and asked Avery to invite Grant over for dinner.

She picked up the school's picture of the girls and their men. Nick was beaming with pride, his arms wrapped around both of his daughters. She'd been surprised by how comfortable Grant looked. He'd clearly had a good time. He wasn't as comfortable as Nick, but he adored Sophia. His hand rested on her shoulder while he grinned down at the little girl.

She sighed and returned her focus to the phone. "What am I going to do? I can't let Sophia fall in love with him. If we need to move again, she'll be devastated. She already thinks Grant should be her dad. She can't lose two father figures in one year."

"So don't lose him. Figure it out as you go."

If she hadn't been feeling so down, Avery might have laughed. Brad had never hesitated with women. He jumped in, feet first, and dealt with any fallouts later. He'd never juggled his own desires with the needs of a child. "I can't do that."

"Take it one day at a time. Save me a seat at Thanksgiving. I'll talk to the lawyer again and rustle up more money. We're going to save the house and have the best small-town Christmas you've ever seen. You'll be stuck living with me all winter. You can worry about Grant once we pay the tax bill. Deal?"

Avery glanced at the Daddy Donut Day photos again. She wiped a few tears from her eyes. There wasn't any time to cry; Sophia would be home from school soon. "One day at a time," she repeated. "See you at Thanksgiving."

Chapter Twenty

Grant

Grant glanced at Avery while they waited for the Kindness Committee meeting to start. Even though she was sitting right next to him, she seemed miles away.

He bumped his knee against hers and gave her a small smile. "I had fun at Daddy Donut Day. I hope the girls didn't have too much sugar. How was Sophia at school today?"

Avery gave him a smile back, but it didn't light up her face the way he'd hoped. "Sophia was fine. She lives for refined carbohydrates. Give her two hours of sleep and a bowl of sugary cereal, and she's ready for the day. I wish I had half of her energy."

Grant laughed. Sophia sure had a lot of energy. He needed a hearty breakfast and two cups of coffee to leave his house each morning.

When had that happened? He'd had as much energy as Sophia when he was a kid. He'd slowed down a bit when he started his own business. But come to think of it, he'd been shouldering adult-sized responsibilities since he was in high school.

Avery hadn't taken care of her parents or grandfather the way he cared for his mom, but neither one of them had an easy childhood. He prayed this wouldn't be the case for Sophia, too. The girl deserved a few carefree years.

Pastor Rick walked to the table and clapped his hands, pulling Grant's focus back to the room. "Good evening, everyone. Thank you for coming. It's a lot harder to get people back for the second meeting. You're the type of volunteers I need—the ones who keep coming back and making a difference."

He paused, looking each member in the eyes. Grant was surprised to realize the pastor was right. There were fewer people compared to the last time. Less than a dozen people sat around the table, including Harry, the silver-haired man who was friends with Avery's grandfather.

Still, Pastor Rick smiled warmly at those who remained. "We'll be forming a board soon. Tonight is our working committee, and we'll need volunteers to work. But we'll also need an official board to approve projects. I hope each of you will consider joining the board. But enough about that for now!" He pointed across the table at Grant. "I want to recognize our first team to finish a project. Grant and Avery, will you stand up?"

Grant stood up reluctantly. He didn't enjoy extra attention. They hadn't built Mary's ramp for a pat on the back; they'd finished it to help someone.

Still, he turned to offer Avery a hand as she stood. "It wasn't a big deal," he said. "I'm glad we could help. Mary should be able to live at home for a long time, and the ramp only took a few hours."

Pastor Rick nodded and gestured for them to sit down. "Thank you. That's the attitude we need! Mary said you did a great job."

He walked around the table, handing a packet of paper to every person. "These are our budget goals for the year. We can't do a lot without money. The wood and labor for Mary's ramp was donated. We won't always be so lucky. We also need cash to hand out gas cards and food vouchers, or buy clothing for people after a house fire. These things cost money."

He stopped talking and turned to the back of the room. Grant looked up and saw Brook walking through the door. She grinned at her friends and claimed the only empty seat across the table.

She nodded at Pastor Rick. "Sorry I'm late. My last delivery took longer than expected. What did I miss?"

Pastor Rick handed her a copy of the budget. "You're just in time. We're talking about ways to raise money. We might have great ideas about helping the community, but we're limited by our budget." He stood behind Brook and placed his hand on her shoulder. "If you haven't met Brook, I'll let her introduce herself. She came to me on Sunday with some fundraising ideas."

Brook stood up to introduce herself. Her entire frame was tense and wired with what Grant assumed was excitement. After telling everyone that she owned the local bakery and had been born and raised in the area, she moved on to her fundraising idea. "We need something big, right? It's got to be splashy. It's got to attract lots of people, and it's got to make those people open their wallets and donate to our cause."

Grant stifled a snort. Open their wallets, huh? Brook always got straight to the point.

She gave Grant a pointed look, then continued. "We need something splashy, like a community carnival. People want something to do while the tourists are gone, even if it's a little cold outside. The town has nothing to do between the lighthouse festival and Christmas. We can combine the carnival with Avery's idea. I'm suggesting a small festival, with food and crafts for sale outdoors. Inside the hall, we'll host a three-hour Zumbathon! You can leave when you need to, but the music won't stop and neither will the fun. A twenty-dollar donation gets you in the door. Stay for an hour, or stay for the entire time."

Harry raised his hand. "We talked about Zoom Gone Wrong at the last meeting. Are the dancers willing to help us?"

Brook grinned and pointed to herself. "You're looking at the newest Zumba instructor in Sunset Cove. I talked to the other instructors, and they're happy to help."

"As long as I don't have to dance, I'm game," Grant said.

"That's a great idea." Brook nodded. "Let's keep Grant from dancing."

Everyone around the table started laughing. Harry wiped tears of laughter from his eyes before he stood up and turned toward Brook. "Sign me up," he said, pointing at her with his cane. "I'll dance for ten hours." He sauntered around the room, shuffling in circles, before he lifted Brook out of his chair to join him.

Grant turned to Avery and shook his head. "It's only the second meeting. Shouldn't the dancing wait until the committee Christmas party?" He watched with concern as Avery's face paled at the mention of Christmas. "Are you okay?"

"I'm fine. I'm just not sure what we'll be doing at Christmas." She was interrupted by her phone ringing. Her brow creased with worry. "Sorry. My phone was on silent. The only call that should go through is Emma, since she's watching Sophia. I've got to take this."

She slipped out the door, only to return moments later. "I've got to leave. My daughter is sick."

Grant stood and rushed to her side. "Should I come with you?"

"It's fine," she said, motioning him back toward the table. "I'm going to meet Emma at home. I can walk. It's only a few blocks."

"Don't be silly." He pulled out his truck keys and placed them in her hand. "Leave the keys in the ignition. Park in your driveway. I'll walk to your house when we're done here."

She nodded and lifted herself on her toes to give him a quick kiss on the cheek. Then she was gone.

As soon as the door closed behind her, Brook led her dancing partner back to his seat. "Let's finish this meeting so Grant can get to Avery's house. The Zumba team is prepared to schedule a dance party for the weekend before Thanksgiving. It's not a lot of time, but we can make it work."

"Let's vote on it. All in favor of a community carnival and Zumba, raise your hands." Pastor Rick looked around the room. Every person had raised their hands. "We're all agreed. Brook, is there a sign-up sheet?"

She nodded and pulled a few papers from her bag. "We outlined exactly what's needed. Our instructors will keep the music going and attract people, but we need at least four volunteers at the front door collecting admission. I need people to sell the bakery's cupcakes and muffins. And we're looking for other businesses that might set up a table and donate a portion of their sales."

She passed the paper around the table. Grant signed himself up for the bakery stand, then added Avery's name. They'd worked together at the lighthouse festival. He hoped she wouldn't mind volunteering for the bakery again, as long as Sophia was better.

They all packed up their notebooks and pulled on their jackets. Grant began to walk toward the door when Brook called out.

"Grant, wait. I have to talk to you. Alone."

He frowned, but let the rest of the group pass through the doors first. When everyone was gone, he turned to his friend. "Is everything okay? What do you need?"

All the energy Brook had brought to the meeting drained out of her body. She sunk into the chair closest to her and shook her head. "Nothing's okay. I've been thinking about this for days and I had to tell you. Avery asked me not to, but…"

"Stop," Grant said. "If Avery wants to tell me something, she will. She told you something in confidence because she trusts you. Don't break that trust."

Brook shook her head. "You don't understand. She's in trouble. We have to help her. And I can't help her alone."

Avery had seemed out of it tonight, but he wasn't sure why. He thought they were close enough to not keep secrets. It surprised him to realize that he was a bit hurt. He wished she'd come to him first for help. "I'd do almost anything for her. But if she doesn't want me to know, I'm not sure what I can do."

"She's going to lose the house and leave Sunset Cove."

He turned to stare at his friend. Avery was going to leave again? His heart hurt at the thought. "Why?"

"There was a mix-up in the county tax office. She owes real estate taxes from the past two years. If she can't find the money, they're taking the house at the end of the month."

Suddenly it all made sense: her distance tonight, and her reaction when he mentioned Christmas.

What could he do to help? He let out a whistle as he considered the problem. Taxes in Sunset Cove weren't cheap. They lived in one of the most beautiful towns in New Jersey. The public schools were great. But the town relied on real estate taxes to keep things running.

"That's a huge problem. But she doesn't want me to know, does she?" He felt another sting of betrayal. Even if they were only friends, he'd hoped she would ask for his help. "She might not accept help from me."

"We've got to help her. Make her see sense."

Grant grimaced as her words hit him. Avery had always been an independent woman. She didn't like other people solving her problems. "I'll try. I can talk to her. But it might not go well."

Brook wiped away a stray tear and nodded. "You've got to try. We lost our best friend ten years ago, and we just got her back. We can't lose her again."

Chapter Twenty-One

Avery

Avery brushed the hair off her daughter's feverish forehead and pulled a blanket up to her chin. "I'll be right down the hall," she promised. "I left water on the nightstand in case you get thirsty. Close your eyes and go to sleep."

Her daughter gave a sleepy nod and rolled over in bed. Emma hadn't been kidding when she said Sophia was sick. Her daughter had gone from a perky, talkative first grader to a sick kid in a few hours.

Avery frowned as she thought about her options. She hadn't even picked a local pediatrician yet. She'd need to make some calls in the morning.

Avery closed her daughter's door, leaving it open a crack in case Sophia needed her. She walked down the hall and hesitated at her own bedroom door. It was too early for bed. She was exhausted, but didn't think laying down would lead to any sleep.

So instead of getting ready for bed, she moved toward a door that had stayed closed since they first arrived. She hadn't ventured into her grandfather's office since his passing. It held too many memories of the man who had rescued her and her brother.

But with their future so uncertain, she was out of time. Avery needed to go through the office, search for papers that might help their financial situation, and pack the things she wanted to keep.

She grabbed an empty moving box and started to sort through the room.

She opened the top drawer of her grandfather's desk, not sure what she would find. Nothing unusual here: some pens, pencils, a calculator and a notepad.

The next drawer was more promising. Inside a faded envelope were several savings bonds in her grandfather's name. They didn't seem to be worth much, but they might help. She sent her brother a picture of the bonds before setting them aside.

There wasn't anything exciting hiding in the other desk drawers. She didn't bother packing much away. She wasn't sure where they were moving to next if they couldn't stay, but none of it seemed important enough to keep.

When she opened the filing cabinet, her jaw dropped. Rows and rows of hanging files greeted her. The names on each of the folders confused her. She'd been expecting neat, orderly documents labeled "tax files," or "investments." Instead, the first file she pulled out was labeled "Christmas gifts."

She opened the file and felt her eyes mist with tears. Her grandfather had kept Sophia's last Christmas wish list. Avery had mailed it to her grandfather after he'd asked for gift ideas. He'd gotten most of the items on the list and drove to their condo to deliver them to Sophia.

Avery's heart dropped as she realized how much those gifts must have cost him. His bank accounts had been nearly empty when he died, and he'd bought his great-granddaughter every gift she wanted.

She flipped the page over and squinted at the next document. She was holding another Christmas last, but it wasn't from Sophia. It was from a boy named Tommy Fritzinger, who asked for a garbage truck and pajamas. The next list was from Megan

Townsend. She wanted a doll with real hair and candy to share with her big brother.

A date and time were listed at the bottom of both lists. Avery wondered if that was the time he had delivered the gifts. It seemed like something her grandfather would do. She closed the folder and thought again about how different life would be if she'd stayed in Sunset Cove. She could have been a part of her grandfather's generosity, working together to make their town a better place. Instead, she was on track to lose everything—the house, her friends, and any chance to stay in her hometown.

She glanced over the rest of the files. She'd go through each one individually, but none looked like investments or savings. It wasn't likely this filing cabinet held the answer to their problems. Curious, she returned to the top drawer and pulled out the list of Christmas gifts again.

When the doorbell rang, Avery rushed out of the room. She didn't want the bell to ring a second time and wake Sophia. Peering through the peephole, she was surprised to find Pastor Rick waiting outside.

"I won't be long," he said. "I wanted to check on you and Sophia. Did you need anything?"

"She should be okay. I could use the name of a pediatrician, though."

"Let me ask around. I'll text you a few names tomorrow morning." He gestured toward the files she was holding. "Did I interrupt you?"

Avery frowned and glanced down at her hands. She'd rushed out of her grandfather's office with the folder holding his Christmas lists. She opened the file and spun it toward the pastor. "I'm looking through his old paperwork. I found this list from the year before he died. I never realized he bought gifts for so many children."

Pastor Rick reached out and traced the first child's name. "Clint never wanted anyone to know. He called himself a Secret Santa. He dropped gifts at the church and had me deliver them. Tommy was so thrilled with the garbage truck. I wish Clint had seen the look on Tommy's face when he opened his gift. But that was your grandfather," he said, his voice thick with emotion. "He didn't want credit for anything. He left big shoes to fill."

Pastor Rick took the file from Avery and flipped through the papers. "Now that he's gone, I don't mind you telling you everything he's done. He lived a simple life and didn't like to spend a lot of money on himself—but he played Secret Santa for almost two decades. I haven't been in Sunset Cove for long. I inherited the job of delivering gifts from the last pastor," he chuckled. "Clint should have been the guy wearing the beard. He gave a cafeteria scholarship to a kid at the start of each school year, but he wouldn't take credit for that, either. Your grandfather had me talk to the teachers and find one family who didn't qualify for free meals but couldn't afford to pay for them. He bought that kid's hot lunches for the entire year. No questions asked."

He gently closed the file and handed it back to Avery. "We didn't have enough money to deliver many gifts last year. It was our first Christmas without Clint. I'm hoping we can raise enough at the Zumbathon to continue Secret Santa."

A few more tears escaped down Avery's cheek. Unless they found a lot of money in the next few weeks, she might not have much time in Sunset Cove to talk about Grandpa. "He was a wonderful grandfather, and a great man. I was very lucky."

"You *are* very lucky. And I hope you won't mind me saying this, but if we can help you back on your feet, let us know. You've had a rough year. We're glad you came here to start over."

She looked at the kind pastor and tried to smile. It had indeed been a rough year, and it wasn't over yet. "Thank you."

After Pastor Rick left, she made a list of ways to find money. She could pick up extra shifts at the bakery. It wouldn't be much. She was already working the morning shift and helping with the lunch prep, and the bakery wasn't open in the evening. Still, every dollar counted at this point.

She wrote "sell house" on the list, then crossed it off. It was foolish to hesitate, but she still hadn't called a realtor. The thought made her stomach churn. That was silly, because whether she sold the house or the tax office claimed it, the result would be the same. She would need to leave, and someone else would live here.

Still, selling felt like giving up. She couldn't do that. There were too many people depending on her.

She bowed her head and prayed for a miracle, something she hadn't done in years. It would take a huge leap of faith, and a small miracle, to stay in Sunset Cove.

Chapter Twenty-Two

Avery

Avery paced back and forth on her front porch. Sophia had bounced back quickly from last week's fever. She would be home from school soon, but Grant was stopping by to work on the community carnival. The fundraiser was this weekend and they needed to finalize last-minute details.

Grant pulled up in his pickup truck. He was right on time, as usual.

She waved half-heartedly and thought about all the times he'd picked her up in his old, noisy pickup. His new truck was quiet and a lot bigger. It was a practical choice for work, but the louder truck suited him better.

Did it, though? Grant's edges had smoothed out over the years. He'd grown into a fine man. Any woman would be lucky to have him.

Avery sighed. Her own luck was running out, and she didn't see their relationship going anywhere. Her grandfather's tax bill was a huge complication. Even if they managed to pay the tax bill, she would spend every penny she had. Staying would mean lots of sacrifices and living paycheck-to-paycheck for a while. It wasn't fair to pull Grant along on this bumpy ride.

She held the door open for Grant, then followed him into her grandfather's house. Grant nodded his thanks and headed straight for the kitchen, where he put down an overflowing grocery bag.

"Pastor Rick asked us to make decorations. Can Sophia help us? I think she'd have fun. We'd get the job done faster with three of us."

Avery agreed and cleared some space off the kitchen table. Sophia was obviously in love with Grant, and that worried her. She hadn't wanted the little girl to become attached. It was too risky. Now it was too late. Both of their hearts were on the line, even with their uncertain future. What was she going to do?

Today, she would set aside her mixed emotions and focus on the job in front of her. "We can do that," she said. "Before she gets home, we have to review the list of vendors who agreed to come. We'll need to call and confirm their arrival time."

She sat down at the kitchen table. Grant pulled out the chair next to her. He leaned closer, his eyes skimming over the list. "You've split the list into two pages. I'll take this first page. Should we start now?"

Avery's mind went blank. His nearness made her brain go fuzzy. It wouldn't take much for her to lean an inch closer and place a kiss on his lips.

She jerked backwards in her seat and nodded. What was she thinking? They were friends. No kissing allowed. She cleared her throat. "I'll take the second sheet. I'm going to the living room. You can make your phone calls from the kitchen."

Twenty minutes later, they met back in the kitchen. The calls had gone quickly, and the fundraiser was still on track. Avery's heart felt lighter. With so much unknown in her life, it was nice to make progress on at least one thing, even if it was just a fundraiser for the town.

They sat down at the table again and dumped out Pastor Rick's decorations. Grant sifted through the pile. "We've got a Thanksgiving theme. Lots of leaves, and a few cornucopias. Should be fun."

They worked in silence for a few minutes, gluing pieces of paper together to match the samples they'd been given. Grant set down a finished cornucopia and focused on Avery. "Sophia will be home soon, right?"

"Yes. Her bus will be here in about ten minutes."

"Good. I wanted to talk before she gets home."

Avery's heart beat faster. Grant caused that reaction in her. She hid her fluster with a smile and reached for a few more leaves to finish her decoration. "You can talk now. We've got a whole ten minutes to ourselves."

Grant reached out to still her hands. He stared into her eyes, as if he was searching for answers to questions he hadn't been able to ask. "Sophia is an amazing kid. You're doing a great job raising her."

"Thanks. She's a little confused with the move and changes, but she's grown a lot these past few weeks. I have, too."

Grant gave her hand a squeeze. "I'm proud of how well you're doing. Has the lawyer called about the divorce?"

Avery gently tugged her hand out of his grasp. "Not yet. Why?"

"You know why."

Avery's heart ached as she looked at Grant. Life was so unfair. The perfect guy was sitting right in front of her. He liked her, and he liked her kid, but the timing was awful. She couldn't commit to a relationship while her life was such a mess.

The silence stretched between them. It was clear they were both drawn to each other, but she still needed to think about Sophia. It wasn't fair to string Sophia or Grant along until she knew what was happening.

There was that word again: fair.

Nothing was fair, it seemed. If life was fair, they would have fallen in love back in high school. They could have built a home together, with their family and friends at their side. But no, life wasn't fair. It wasn't easy, either. There was no sense tricking herself into believing otherwise.

"It's...complicated," she said.

"It doesn't have to be. I care about you, Avery."

She sighed and stood up from the table. Needing something to do with her hands, she went to the counter and poured out two mugs of coffee, and spoke while her back was still facing him. "I care about you, too. But it might not be enough. I'm not sure where we'll be in six weeks, let alone six months. I've got more to worry about than the divorce."

"Is it about the house? The tax money?"

Avery spun around, hot coffee sloshing over the mugs and onto the table. She stared at him in shock. She hadn't told many people about her problems, only Brook and Brad. How did he know?

Emotions race through her mind. Surprise and shame fought each other, but anger rose to the top. "You knew, and you didn't say anything. Who told you?"

Grant stood and carefully took the steaming coffee mugs from her hand. He placed them on the counter and grabbed a rag to clean up the spilled drinks. "It's not a rumor going around town, if that's what you're worried about. Brook told me. She's worried about you. I am too. I can loan you some money..."

Avery shook her head and grabbed the rag from Grant's hand. "This is my mess. I can clean it up," she said, not sure if she meant the spilled drinks or her own messy life. "I don't need a man to save me."

Grant held his hands up in surrender. "I'm not trying to save you. We want to help. That's what friends do. They help each other."

She took a deep breath and tried to calm her anger. This wasn't Grant's fault. If anyone was to blame, it was Eric. He'd lied and hid the problem until it was too late. "Yes, I owe taxes on the house.

They're due next month. If I can't find the money, we'll have to move."

"Move? To where?"

Avery shrugged and slumped against the kitchen counter. "I don't know yet. We can't afford a place in Sunset Cove. Prices are crazy around here. If we lose this house to the tax office, we'll need to find something cheaper inland."

Her heart ached as she said those words. She'd just introduced Sophia to the ocean, and they were both falling in love with Sunset Cove and this wonderful man standing here. But what could they do? She wouldn't take Grant's money. She needed to fix this on her own. "I'm sorry. I wasn't trying to lead you on. I can't start a relationship with you right now, or with anyone else."

Grant sighed and nodded. "I didn't think you'd take money, but I'm willing to help. I care about you and Sophia. I'm falling in love with both of you. But I promised not to pressure you, and I won't. Should I leave before Sophia gets here?"

Avery choked back a sob and closed your eyes. He was in love with her? She wished her life was simple, that a boy and a girl could fall in love with no consequences. But life wasn't simple. And they weren't teenagers anymore. She was a single mom, and her little girl was getting far too close to Grant.

It was too late for her own heart, but she couldn't risk her daughter's heart, too. "Yes, it might be better if you left. Leave the crafts. Sophia will help me finish it. I'll get them to Pastor Rick before Saturday."

"That's fine." He pushed in his chair and added his cornucopia to the pile of decorations they'd finished. "I'm giving you some space. But I still want to be friends. Got it? I'm not walking away. I'd never hurt you on purpose."

Avery nodded. Grant stepped onto the front porch and slowly closed the front door behind him. He might not try to hurt her or

Sophia, but she'd done a fine job of hurting him. She watched out the window as his truck pulled away from the curb.

A few moments later, the school bus arrived. Sophia burst through the front door, a flurry of energy and noise that Avery wasn't prepared to deal with.

"Mom! I saw Grant's truck! Was he here?"

"He had to leave, but yes. He was here."

"I made him a card today in school. Want to see it?"

Sophia dug through her bookbag and pulled out a crumpled green card. On the front, she'd drawn countless circles and scrawled out, "Thank you for being my donut dad!"

Avery forced another smile. Her nerves were stretched to the limit, but it wasn't her daughter's fault. It wasn't Grant's fault, either. "Let's set it here, and we can give it to him on Saturday. Okay? We're going to glue some leaves on these decorations tonight."

Sophia cheered and reached for the glue. Avery showed her how to make the first decoration, but her mind wandered as they worked. What had she done? Instead of thanking Grant for his support, she'd pushed him away again. She'd been dragging him along for weeks, letting him take her on not-quite-dates and kiss her on the cheek. Now she was going to lose him, and this house, and everything she'd tried to piece together in Sunset Cove.

She was seriously bad at being a good friend. Maybe she should give up the house and leave. They'd move back to the city, where she had been lonely and isolated. She'd fall back into her old habits, where friendships didn't exist outside PTO night.

The thought made her heart hurt. Her city friends were never available for late-night walks on the beach, or willing to give her a job when she was down on her luck. Her childhood friends had been there when she needed them the most, and she'd pushed them away.

What had she done?

Chapter Twenty-Three

Avery

Avery finished cleaning up the bakery's kitchen, wiping down counters and putting the last of the clean bowls away.

She was normally home by this time. The school day was nearly over. Seaside Cupcakes stayed open late on Fridays to give the weekend tourists a chance to pick out baked goods, but Brook usually handled the afternoon shift alone.

Brook gave the kitchen a final look-over, then nodded and untied her apron. "Are you sure you want to close today? I can lock the doors now, and we can both go home. I'm not expecting a lot of customers. You don't need to keep the bakery open."

Avery waved off her concerns. She took the apron from her boss's hand and tossed it into the laundry pile. "I'm sure. Sophia's sleeping at a friend's house tonight. I'll stay open as long as we have something to sell."

Brook looked at her friend with concern. "You're working too hard."

Avery *was* working hard. She'd come in early every day this week, picking up extra hours to earn a larger paycheck. Today was the last Kindness Committee meeting before the big fundraiser. They would decorate the hall and hang signs for outdoor vendors. Instead of helping with setup, she'd offered to keep the bakery open for Brook.

She didn't enjoy skipping the meeting, but it was too soon to see Grant. They'd barely spoken since their argument. He had texted her twice: once to make sure she was okay, and again to confirm they would sell baked goods together at the fundraiser. He'd kept his tone friendly and light, and kept his promise not to pressure her.

Avery wasn't looking forward to seeing Grant tomorrow. She didn't want to spend the day together, pretending to only be friends. How could she, knowing he loved her? She was falling in love with him, too. It would be tough to be friends with Grant. But she had to try, for Sophia's sake.

"If you're sure." Brook seemed uncertain as she reached for the doorknob. "I'll tell everyone why you're not there tonight. Text me when you leave, so I can add your hours to next week's paycheck." She opened the door, then pulled it shut again and faced her friend. "I heard you broke up with Grant. If I had anything to do with it..."

Avery cut her off with a shake of her head. "We weren't dating, so we didn't break up. Besides, it's not your fault. I shouldn't have expected you to keep the tax bill a secret. It wasn't fair to you."

"You shouldn't have to deal with this alone. It's a big problem."

"I'm not alone. I've got my brother. We'll figure this out."

"You will. But you can still ask for help."

Avery's eyes watered as she rushed over to give Brook a hug. "Thank you for taking me back. I haven't been a great friend since I left town. I won't take any of my friends for granted again. What would I do without you?"

Brook pulled back from the hug to smile at her friend. "You're not going to find out. We're here for you."

·♥·♥·♥·♥·♥·

Four hours later, Avery sat alone in a dark house. She'd admitted defeat when the bakery had no customers for a full hour.

Now she sat in her grandfather's guest room. She'd stashed their extra boxes in a corner, hoping to unpack them when she had time. Now time was running out. They could be homeless soon.

Even though she'd done the whole packing-and-moving thing last month, it seemed different. Last time, they'd been driving toward a fresh start and a second chance at happiness. Now they were being pushed away from that second chance. Avery would do her best to give Sophia a soft landing, but she wasn't sure where life would take them next. She prayed her little girl wouldn't lose her sunny outlook and easy smile in the process.

Her ringtone pulled Avery out of deep thought. She reached for the phone and saw her brother's number on the screen.

She mustered up a fake smile, determined to make her brother not worry about her. She'd learned that if your face looked cheerful, your voice sounded cheerful. It was the best way to hide sadness or loneliness. Her smile slipped as she realized how often she hid her loneliness.

"Hi Brad!" she chirped, in her best impression of a chipper voice. "Are you packing your bags yet?"

"Almost done. I wanted to call with an update. My boss said there's no work 'till spring. I'm sorry."

Avery's stomach twisted in a knot. She hadn't expected Brad's boss to come through. It would have been nice, though. Brad had worked there for years, but he was still a lowly employee. Avery suspected he could have done better under a different boss—someone who treated him more fairly, with regular hours.

"It's okay." The cheer slipped from her voice, and she focused on sounding happier. "I worked extra hours this week, and we've still got time. Once you get here for Thanksgiving, I'm sure we'll figure this out."

Avery wanted to believe her own words, but she wasn't sure at this point.

Her brother didn't seem to notice her fake cheerfulness. "Since I'm not working, I can stay with you after Thanksgiving. You need Uncle Brad. I make everyone more jolly."

Avery let out a genuine laugh. She missed her big brother. He knew how to make her smile. "You're the life of the party, that's for sure. When will you get here?"

"I'm leaving Wednesday afternoon. Does that work? I'll be there before Sophia's bedtime."

"That's perfect. I'm making the turkey at my house, and my friends are bringing the side dishes and desserts. You won't have too much to do, but it would be nice to have company while I'm cooking. Sophia's excited to have her uncle here for Thanksgiving. You can distract her for a bit while I'm prepping the turkey."

"Sounds like a plan. I haven't been able to spoil her in a long time. I'm looking forward to it."

Avery groaned and shook her head, then realized her brother couldn't see her through the phone. "No spoiling until we figure out where we're living," she said. She paused as the statement sent another pang through her heart. "We don't need extra toys to pack up and move."

"I will come prepared to play with her existing dolls and teacups."

He kept an edge of humor in his voice, and Avery did her best to follow his lead. "Very sensible. I'm sure my friends would love to watch you on the floor of our living room, having tea with all of her dolls."

Brad let out a loud laugh. "Who's coming to Thanksgiving, anyway? Anyone I know? And are they joining us for tea?"

Avery rattled off the names of her friends. "You know Brook, of course. I'm not sure if you've met the other girls. We're all single and didn't want anyone to be alone for Thanksgiving. But we took a vote and accepted you into our group."

Brad cleared his throat. "Thanksgiving for single people. Is this a matchmaking event?"

Now it was Avery's turn to laugh. "No, nothing like that. We've all decided friends are as important as family during the holidays. None of us have family nearby. Or at least I didn't, until you decided to visit. I am glad you're coming, though. You should meet my friends."

"Sure, sounds like fun. Will Grant be there, too?"

Avery hesitated. "No, he won't be at Thanksgiving."

"Will I see him at all? It would be good to catch up with him."

She paused again as she considered how to word her response. Would he see Grant? Probably. It was hard to avoid people in a small town like Sunset Cove. Avery was surprised she hadn't run into Grant yet since their argument. They would both be at the fundraiser. But after tomorrow? She wanted to stay friends with him, but it might be safer to limit their interactions to random run-ins at the grocery store.

She thought about their literal run-in last month at Sunset Market. Back when she was eager for a fresh start in Sunset Cove. She would give almost anything to go back to those first days, when she thought they were putting down firm roots in her hometown.

Now she wasn't sure what would happen. If they couldn't keep her grandfather's house, the best they could hope for was a cheap apartment nearby. It wouldn't be an easy find. But she wasn't giving up yet. She had ten more days and planned to use every one of those days to fight for their home.

Should she have given up on Grant so easily? The question hit her hard. She let the phone slide away from her face. "I made a mistake," she whispered.

"What's that? I can't hear you." Brad's reply was barely audible with the phone so far away.

She jerked back to their conversation and pulled the phone back to her face. "I made a mistake. Grant and I had an argument. I told him we should just be friends, but I pushed him too far away. I don't think you'll be seeing him around the house. And that's my fault."

Brad sighed. She hadn't seen her brother in ages, but she imagined him rubbing his hands across his face, the way he always did when he was considering his next words.

"I'm not the best person to give relationship advice. But I lost someone I cared about because I was afraid to admit my feelings for her. I was confused, so I friend-zoned her."

Avery's eyebrows rose. Brad never hesitated to ask a woman out. He never formed close relationships, either. He liked easy dates with uncomplicated women. She'd never seen him in a relationship for more than a few weeks. "When did this happen? You never told me about it."

"You were too young to talk about it. I missed out on a great thing because I wasn't man enough to admit my mistakes."

"So... I should be more manly?" she asked.

Brad barked out a laugh. "Please, no. It's okay to make mistakes. Just don't let them hold you back. If you made a mistake with Grant, talk to him."

Avery nodded thoughtfully, then stood up in surprise when she noticed the time.

"I'll keep that in mind, but I've got to go. We're waking up early for the fundraiser. I'll see you in a few days?"

"See you in a few days. I'll be the uncle drinking pretend tea."

Chapter Twenty-Four

Grant

Grant walked into the community room of Grace Lutheran Church. It was quiet now, but not for long.

Up near the front, Brook pointed to different walls and helped people hang signs on the walls. When she noticed Grant, she cheered and ran toward him. "You're here! Thanks for coming so early. I wanted to talk before Avery gets here."

"Why? What do you have planned?" he asked, raising his eyebrows.

"Don't blame me. It was Pastor Rick's idea. We're raising money for a fund in her grandfather's name, and wanted it to be a surprise."

Brook dragged Grant over to a table with a framed picture of Clint Brown, Avery's grandfather. A sign stood next to the photo: *The Clint Brown Kindness Fund: Donate today!*

She waved toward the table with Clint's name and picture. "You were going to sell cupcakes, but you should work here instead. It will give Avery a chance to see what her grandfather's done for this town."

"Are you sure she'll be okay with that?" Grant asked, staring at Clint's picture. "She doesn't have any money to donate. Avery might feel guilty."

"We can donate more than money, remember? Pastor Rick said our time is priceless. Standing behind this table will be a huge help. Please. Convince her to do this."

Grant sighed and nodded, then watched as his friend bounced back to the front of the room to lead the rest of their volunteers. He hoped Avery wouldn't be mad about their change of plans.

They hadn't spoken often this week, but he'd messaged her a few times about the fundraiser. He wanted to show up at her house again with dinner or another splashy bouquet. Give her a hug and promise that she would always have a home in Sunset Cove, even if she couldn't afford to keep her grandfather's home. But he'd held back.

His heart ached as he realized how badly he wanted to build a life with Avery. His own house was too small, too quiet. He'd promised to give Avery space and time, but it was killing him inside. He was ready to settle down.

He shook his head and checked the clock on the wall. Avery would be here in a few minutes. He tried to distract himself by straightening the tablecloth on their display table and moving the donation jar from one side to the other.

Nope, not helping. He couldn't keep his mind off Avery.

He was daydreaming again when Pastor Rick surprised him, walking up behind Grant and putting an arm around his shoulders. "It's almost time! Do you need anything before people arrive?"

"I'm all set. I just hope Avery is ready for this," Grant said, turning to look at Clint's picture again.

"She will be. We're all here for her today, and in the future. She's going through a lot right now, but don't worry. We won't let your girls become homeless."

Grant's eyes flew to the pastor. "You know about the house?"

"Of course I do. I know everything that happens in this town. I hear things."

Grant crossed his arms and considered the pastor in front of him. "What else have you heard?"

"I heard you're upset about Avery leaving. Is that right?"

"Of course I'm upset. Her coming home is the best thing that's happened to me." Grant's voice cracked. He cleared his throat, alarmed to realize how close he was to tears.

The pastor nodded. "She's a special woman. Her little girl is special, too."

"What can I do? Once her grandfather's house is gone, she'll have no reason to stay."

"You're a smart man. Convince her to stay," Pastor Rick said, raising his eyebrows. "We might not save her house, but we can make sure she has choices in Sunset Cove. Those choices won't matter if she leaves. Give her a reason to stay here."

"How do I do that? She left town ten years ago and didn't look back. She won't stay now."

"Did you ask her to stay? Or did you watch her walk away, cursing your luck and believing it was out of your control?"

Grant hesitated. He *hadn't* asked Avery to stay, even as a friend. He hadn't told her she was special or asked her out. He hadn't kissed her under the stars after graduation, even when Avery was about to leave. It was one of his biggest regrets.

Pastor Rick nodded. "That's what I thought. I'm getting out of your hair now. First, let me tell you about the man who prayed for help during a flood. God sent that man a rescue boat. What do you think he did?"

"He got in the boat, I hope."

"He did not. He told the boat owner he didn't need help. God would save him. He kept praying for a miracle, refusing help from one person after another until he drowned." Pastor Rick tilted his head to the side and studied Grant. "Sometimes the miracle we're waiting for is right in front of us. Don't wait for a sign. Do yourself a favor and climb into the boat. Ask Avery to stay."

The pastor walked away, singing "Row, Row, Row Your Boat" quietly as he went.

Grant shook his head. He'd never met anyone like Pastor Rick before. Maybe he should check out the man's Sunday sermons.

His phone vibrated as Brook turned on the stereo, filling the hall with energetic music. Grant yanked the phone out of his pocket. He gave a silent prayer Avery wouldn't cancel on him.

Avery

> Sorry, running late. Can you handle the cupcakes without me?

> Take your time.
> But don't miss it. Brook's playing your favorite songs.

Avery

> Be there in 30 minutes.

Grant let out a breath he hadn't realized he'd been holding. She wasn't canceling. She was just late.

He turned his focus to the people coming into the hall. A few came to his table, drawn to the sign for the Clint Brown Kindness Fund. Glancing down, he noticed a pile of flyers ready to hand out. They were stacked next to a donation box.

Grant didn't expect his table to be busy. The Kindness Committee was already charging twenty dollars for every adult who came to the Zumbathon. Few people would give a second donation.

To his surprise, his table had a slow but steady flow of visitors.

A small boy gave him five dollars. He explained that Clint had bought his lunch when he'd forgotten his money at home. "I wanted to pay him back today," he said, grinning at Grant. "He wouldn't take the money from me last year."

An older woman stuffed twenty dollars into the box. Clint had given her grandson a new bookbag two years ago, she said. Money had been tight, but Clint made sure her grandson had a clean bookbag filled with supplies.

Brook stopped to donate a hundred-dollar bill from an anonymous donor, then added her own handful of twenty-dollar bills. "He always tipped well," she said, giving Grant a wink.

He watched with amazement as one person after the other gave what they could, all in memory of Avery's grandfather.

When Pastor Rick came to check on him a few minutes before Avery was due to arrive, he nodded as he opened the locked box. "I thought it would fill up quickly. Clint Brown was a generous man. He often thought more about others than he did of himself." The pastor pulled the money out of the box and added it to a bank bag. They would keep donations in the church safe. "We're giving the town a chance to thank him one last time. I suspect you're going to be very busy today."

Grant nodded. He hoped Avery would be here soon. She deserved to see the town's support.

Chapter Twenty-Five

Avery

Avery fumbled with the heavy basket in her trunk, struggling to hold the handle with one hand while she closed the truck lid. Letting Sophia sleep at Emma's had been a mistake. They'd been rushing all morning. Now they were almost an hour late.

"Honey, can you grab my purse? It's on the front seat."

"I can get your purse! And your coat! There's music playing," her daughter exclaimed. "Are you going to dance with me?"

"I'll try, Sophia. I don't know how busy I'll be. But you can dance with Brook the whole time."

Her daughter nodded, satisfied with Avery's answer. She skipped alongside her mother, letting the purse and coat swing with each step.

They passed through the carnival. Avery marched ahead as Sophia slowed down to take in the scene. There would be time to explore later, but right now, they needed to get inside.

The smell of hearty barbecue and funnel cake made her mouth water. To her surprise, crowds were already filling the church parking lot. Brook had been right. Even the chill of November couldn't keep hungry people away.

When they finally reached the community room, Avery spotted Brook and waved her friend over. "Sorry I'm late. Sophia didn't want to leave her friend's house. Then she spilled juice all over her clothes. It's been a crazy morning."

"No problem. The music just started, so your timing is perfect. I'll take the basket," she said, hefting it off Avery's arm. "The raffle is back here. I'll be up front with Sophia, leading the crowd. But there's been a change of plans for your table."

"Oh! Is something wrong with the cupcakes? I should have called to check. Can I fix something for you?"

"The cupcakes are fine," Brook said, pointing at a table where Emma and Kerry were selling baked goods as fast as they could slip them into paper bags. "We need you at another table. Give me a minute."

Her friend lugged the basket to the raffle table, where another volunteer greeted her and taped a number to her donation. Avery looked around the hall in confusion. Where was Grant? Why weren't they selling cupcakes together?

She finally found Grant as Brook walked them across the busy floor. He was standing behind a table talking to the grocery store owners. He had a big smile on his face, like he was eager to have this conversation with the Hollands. Grant was so good with people. He always made them feel important.

Her heart ached when she saw him. She would miss him so much if they had to leave.

There were only a few days left to pay her grandfather's bills. She'd been working hard, but they still didn't have enough.

As Mr. and Mrs. Holland turned away from the table, they spotted Avery and beckoned her over. She smiled and waved as she slowly moved through the crowd to join them.

Mrs. Holland embraced her in a warm hug, giving an extra squeeze as she leaned in to speak over the loud music. "We were hoping you would be here. I'm so glad someone thought to include your grandfather. If he were still alive, he'd be at the front of the room, cheering people on."

Avery pulled out of the hug and stared at Mrs. Holland. "They included my grandfather? What do you mean?"

The woman gestured toward Grant's table. Avery's mouth dropped when she saw the picture of Grandpa sitting on the table. She stared at the picture for a moment, overcome with emotion. When she could finally speak, she turned back to Mrs. Holland and gave her another hug. "I wasn't expecting this, but it's a nice surprise. You're right. Grandpa would have been at the front of the room. He was the best cheerleader."

Mrs. Holland gave Avery one last pat on the back, then grinned. "The basket raffle is calling my name. It's for a good cause, right? I hope I win the basket filled with wine vouchers."

Avery was still laughing as the couple shuffled away through the crowd. She slid around the table and bumped shoulders with Grant. "I guess we're not serving cupcakes?"

Grant searched her eyes, gauging her reaction. "No cupcakes. Pastor Rick thought it would be good to see what an impact your grandfather had on Sunset Cove. Are you okay with this? I didn't enjoy surprising you. I wasn't told about the table until today."

Avery watched as a little girl ran up to their cash box and smiled shyly as she dropped in a few quarters. A moment later, an older man step forward, nodded, and stuffed a hundred-dollar bill into the box. Avery's eyes widened. "It's not what I was expecting at all, but it's wonderful. I'm glad my grandfather can help this town one last time."

She took a deep breath and turned to face Grant. "I also owe you an apology. I didn't mean to kick you out of the house last week. It wasn't your fault Brook told you about our problems. You meant well."

"I'm still willing to help, if you'll let me."

Avery leaned on Grant's shoulder and sighed. "I know. But I've got to do this on my own. No matter what the future holds, I don't want Sophia to think she needs a man to fix her problems."

He wrapped his arm around Avery and gave her a quick squeeze. "It's okay to need help. Some problems are too big for one person. That's an important lesson for Sophia to learn, too."

The friends stood in silence, watching the crowd jump and move to the music. *This is amazing*, Avery thought. *Look at those people moving as one. They're working together to help the town, too.*

After weeks of stress, it was wonderful to turn off her thoughts and sway to the pulse of the beat. Grant reached out and took her hands, pulling her into a crazy dance. They weren't following the group, but that was okay. She laughed as they made up their own moves.

She'd missed Grant so much. Their easy friendship, the way they could have fun doing almost anything. How could she live without him?

Pastor Rick startled Avery out of her thoughts when by tapping her shoulder. He yelled to be heard over the music. "Sorry, I didn't mean to sneak up on you. How's it going?"

Grant eased his arm off Avery's waist and grinned. "It's going well. You should empty the money box again. It was a great idea to set up a fund in Clint's name. Give him one last chance to make a difference."

Pastor Rick shook his head as he shoveled dollar bills from the box to his money bag. "If I have my way, this won't be the last time Clint makes a difference. I'd like to make it an annual fund."

Avery smiled. She wrapped her arms around her waist, feeling empty now that Grant wasn't dancing with her. "I like that. I'm not sure we'll be here next year, though. We might be moving. But we will stay in touch."

Grant stiffened next to her, like her words had sent a shock through his body.

Pastor Rick's expression didn't change. "Stay in touch? I was hoping you'd be on the Kindness board. Don't tell me you've forgotten already."

Avery's head spun with his reminder. Join the Kindness board? Continue her grandfather's mission? She wasn't sure how that would be possible. It would take a miracle just to keep her in Sunset Close. "I'll think about it. I'm juggling a lot right now, and I'm not sure where we'll be in a few months."

Grant quietly cleared his throat. "I'd like you to be here, in Sunset Cove. Even if you can't live in your grandfather's house."

She turned to face him. A single tear fell down her face. "I don't want to leave," she breathed, her voice barely audible over the music.

"Don't leave," he said, almost as quietly. "Stay. We'll work it out."

"You two need a break." Pastor Rick nudged Avery and Grant out from behind the table. "Why don't you grab a drink? Maybe take a walk outside where it's quieter. I'll watch the table for a few minutes. Take your time."

"But I just got here," Avery said, confused.

To her surprise, Grant nodded and picked up their coats. "I've been here for a while. Take a break with me."

Grant grabbed two waters from a cooler and traded them for a five-dollar bill. He put his hand on her back and ushered her out into the cool autumn air.

"It's a beautiful day for a carnival," she said, twisting the water bottle in her hands. "My grandfather would be proud of what Pastor Rick has done here. I didn't realize Grandpa had inspired so many people. I should have been paying closer attention."

"Clint did all of his work quietly. He didn't want a lot of recognition." Grant shook his head and gently touched his hand to Avery's face. He pulled her chin upward to look into her eyes. "He would be proud of you, too. You're working to give your kid a better life. Just like he worked to help everyone in Sunset Cove."

"I'm only doing what he did for me," she argued, stepping away from his touch. "I'm not doing anything special. He helped dozens of people. I'm hardly helping the entire town."

"You're doing an amazing job, and it sounds like Pastor Rick will help you with the next-generation town hero thing. If you're willing to take it on."

"It's not that simple..."

"Your grandfather wouldn't want money to drive you away. He'd be so happy you came back," Grant said fiercely, gesturing toward the town. "He would be thrilled that you're living in his house. Clint loved visiting you, no matter where you lived. But you belong here. In Sunset Cove."

"I don't want to leave. I just don't know how I can stay."

"We'll find a way." Grant brushed the hair away from Avery's face. "I want you to stay. I want to help you and Sophia. Not because I'm a man and need to fix this for you, but because I love both of you. That's what people do when they care. They work together."

He leaned in and brushed a soft kiss on her cheek. After a moment, he backed away toward the door. "I shouldn't be pushing you. I'm going back inside. It's your choice whether you stay in town or leave. But I'll always be your friend, and hopefully something more."

Avery watched him walk away. Once the door closed behind him, she reached up and touched the place where he'd kissed her. Every emotion she'd ever felt in this town came bubbling to the surface. Fear, regret, and love simmered inside of her, each emotion fighting for attention.

What did she want? Was she willing to leave a person like Grant? Or would she take her brother's advice and speak up before it was too late?

Grant was her best friend, and he'd told her a few times now that he wanted more than friendship. She wanted that too, she realized.

She'd let a man guide and control her once before, and look where it had gotten her. She could be homeless by next month, all thanks to Eric's need to manage her entire life. But Grant was nothing like her ex-husband.

She may have returned to Sunset Cove alone, with no other options. But now she had Grant and Brook. She had Emma, Kerry, and other friends, too. It shocked her to realize how much had changed in the last few weeks.

She was still a single mom, of course. Her money problems wouldn't fix themselves. But with a burst of clarity, Avery realized she could never leave Sunset County again. Her heart was here, along with her family. She raced toward the door, eager to tell Grant she was going to fight to make their relationship work. She hoped it wasn't too late.

She had a fundraiser to run. But that wasn't all she had waiting for her. She had a life to build here in Sunset Cove.

Chapter Twenty-Six

Grant

Grant paced behind the table, watching more people donate to Clint's fund. Brook stood at the front of the room, leading the crowd through an upbeat song. He couldn't believe the energy in the room. The space was filled with music, drowning out every conversation and filling his soul with sound.

People clapped as the song ended and a new Zumba instructor took the stage. As much as he wanted to join in, Grant couldn't find the energy to cheer.

He wasn't sure how he felt right now. Grant knew without a doubt that he'd told the truth outside—he was in love with Avery Brown. He'd been in love with her for years. It had taken the threat of losing her again to make him realize it, but he'd gotten there in the end.

He'd come a long way from his teenage years, when he was too afraid to ask Avery out on a date. Still, he worried he was too late.

People continued to stream into the room, eager to raise money for the community. But without Avery by his side, he felt utterly alone. He searched through the crowd again, wondering if Avery would come back inside or just go home. Maybe he'd pushed her too hard.

Pastor Rick put a hand on his arm. "Don't be so tense. You asked her to stay?"

"I did."

"What did she say?"

"She doesn't want to leave. But she didn't say much else."

Pastor Rick clapped Grant on the back with a grin. "She didn't say 'no.' That's a start. And I think your day will get better."

Grant gave him a puzzled look, then realized Avery was walking toward the table. She'd come back. Warmth filled his chest as he realized how happy that made him. But what if she'd come to say goodbye?

Pastor Rick didn't seem concerned, though. He only grinned wider. "I've got a good feeling. Seems like you did a fine job convincing her to stay." He flipped open the cash box on their table again and slid more money into his bank bag.

Distracted as he was, it shocked Grant to see how many bills they had collected. There were even a few checks stuffed inside the box.

"I'll be in the church office. I'd like to tell everyone how much money we raised today. This is going to make a big difference in our town. But I suspect you're making a difference in your life today, too," Pastor Rick said, nodding at Grant. "Good luck."

Grant took a deep breath as the pastor walked away, letting it out slowly as he watched Avery cross the room. She threaded through the crowd, stopping to laugh with a few friends as they bumped into each other. Then she looked his way.

Time seemed to stop as they locked eyes. But while Grant expected the laughter to fall from her face, she kept smiling. Maybe Pastor Rick was right to think good things were about to happen.

She said a few more words to her friends, then moved toward their table again. It took a few minutes for her to finish crossing the busy room. To Grant, it seemed like a lifetime of waiting.

"You're back. Is everything okay?" he asked cautiously, moving toward Avery. He stopped just out of reach. He desperately wanted to hold her, but still wanted to give her space.

"I'm okay. In fact, I'm better than ever." She took a step toward him and looked into his eyes. "We're staying in Sunset Cove. I've only got a week left to save my grandfather's house, but I'm not giving up. I deserve the chance to stay here. *We* deserve a chance."

Grant's heart nearly burst with joy. "We?"

"Us. You, me, and Sophia. If you're still willing to wait until the divorce is finalized."

He wrapped his arms around Avery and lifted her off the ground. "You're worth waiting for. I will do everything in my power to help you stay," he promised.

"I'm sorry I left after high school."

"You needed to leave. You had big dreams. If you'd stayed, you would have wondered what was waiting for you outside our town."

Avery made a face, but nodded. "Now I know what's out there. Plenty of people find happiness in the city, but I wasn't one of them. I missed home so badly it hurt. I just never had a chance to come back. Eric always kept me away."

Anger surged through Grant when Avery mentioned her ex-husband's name, but he tried to hide how much Eric affected him. "You're here now. We're going to help you stay. What can I do?"

Avery huffed out of breath and shook her head. "I'm not sure. I emptied my savings account, and my brother did the same. We're *not* taking money from you. We're halfway there, and there's still one more week to find the money."

"You'll find it," Grant said confidently.

Avery shook her head, unconvinced. "We might not. That's okay. We'll use what we have to find another house. It might not be in town. We'll stay as close as possible. In the meantime, Brook said we can use her spare bedroom."

"I've got a spare bedroom, too," Grant said softly. He thought about the room he'd made for his mother. She'd passed away before he could move her in. He'd kept the spare bed and dressers. It was a reminder to always make space for family.

Was that what Avery was now? Was she family, his best friend, or something more? He frowned and pushed the question from his mind. Today wasn't the time to worry about labels. He would celebrate the fact that Avery was staying in Sunset Cove.

Avery looks surprised at the offer of his spare bedroom. Then she shook her head again. "I wouldn't be comfortable staying in your house with Sophia. Not while I'm still married."

"That's understandable. We'll take things slowly." He itched to pull her in close again, but settled for tugging her an inch nearer.

To his surprise, Avery reached up and touched his face. She leaned in closely. He expected a kiss on the cheek. Instead, she gave him a soft kiss on the lips.

Grant wrapped his arms around her in a hug, gently this time. "I'll give you as much time as you need. Just don't walk away, okay? No leaving town. We'll wait this out together."

"Together," she agreed.

They turned to the front of the room as the music stopped. Up front, someone was tapping on a microphone to get their attention.

"Excuse me. Hello. Can you all hear me?" Pastor Rick gripped the microphone in one hand, juggling a stack of papers in his other arm. "I've got some announcements to make. Can everyone hear me?"

Brook rushed to his side and took the papers from his arms. She leaned in to speak to him. He nodded, then picked up one piece of paper off the pile. "Brook says you can hear me. First, I wanted to thank everyone for coming today. I'm glad to see the Sunset Cove community supporting our neediest residents. This is an amazing place to live."

Grant felt a surge of pride for his town. As he stood listening with his arm wrapped around Avery, he gave her a little squeeze and grinned at her. Yes, this was a pretty amazing town.

The pastor held up the paper in his hands. "Before you leave today, I want you to know what a difference you've made. By walking in the door and paying for admission, you raised more than three thousand dollars."

The crowd clapped. A few people nodded at each other, as if this number impressed them. Grant had to admit it was an impressive amount.

"Seaside Cupcakes sold hundreds of cupcakes, cookies, and muffins," the pastor continued. "Brook didn't price anything. She asked you to pay with your heart, and you did. The bake sale raised seven thousand dollars."

Grant grinned as Avery raised her arms and cheered, pointing at her friend.

The pastor cleared his throat before speaking into the microphone again. "There is one man who should be celebrating with us today. Clint Brown was always the first person to arrive when someone needed help. He'd open his wallet, his schedule, and his heart to anyone in this town."

Grant looked down at Avery. She had a rueful expression on her face as she nodded. She wasn't crying yet, but Grant suspected tears weren't far away. He hoped the town had been generous in Clint's name.

The pastor continued, "Clint was the most generous man I've ever met, but this town's generosity has floored me. You've done him proud. I'm pleased to announce that the Clint Brown Kindness Fund raised an additional thirteen thousand dollars."

The crowd gasped.

The pastor nodded. "It's only fitting that your outstanding generosity was used to honor an outstanding man. Ladies and gentlemen, that's a *lot* of school lunches and handicapped ramps. We changed lives today."

Tears streamed down Avery's face. Grant knew the pastor had aimed high with this fundraiser, but he never thought they'd raise this much money.

It seemed Clint Brown had been the deciding factor. The Brown family touched people's hearts. Grant wrapped his other arm around Avery in a hug. "You did good. Your grandfather would be proud. And I think he's here today, among all these people. Don't you?"

Avery gave a shuddering breath against his chest. Hiding her head, she nodded.

He didn't make her say anything more. Just knowing she would stay, and that they'd both found a new purpose in town, was enough for today.

Chapter Twenty-Seven

Avery

—ele—

Avery used her sweater sleeve to pat her eyes dry. It had been an incredible night. Now the team needed to tear down decorations and clean the room.

She made small talk with Grant as they carefully rolled up the signs and packed away her grandfather's picture. The Clint Brown Kindness Fund had been wildly successful. She hoped her grandfather was happy. He hadn't liked to brag or accept recognition, but he was never afraid to stand up and encourage others.

Pastor Rick came over to greet her as she snapped the lid on a tote. "We had a good turnout. We'll be able to help lots of people, thanks to you and the rest of the team."

Avery shrugged off the compliment. "I hardly did anything. It was your idea. You gather people, and you inspire them. You bring out the best in everyone."

He grinned at her. "Does that mean you'll join the Kindness board? We need folks who understand this town and what it needs. We need people like you and Grant."

"I'd be happy to," Avery said. "What do you think, Grant? No pressure. We don't have to do this together."

"If you're in, I'm in," he said easily. "I'm ready to hire a few more employees at Grant Construction. Fewer nights and weekends on the job. More time with the people I love."

"That's the spirit." Pastor Rick held out his hand to give them both a firm handshake. "Our first meeting is Monday night. We'll have babysitting, so bring Sophia. She'll have fun."

Avery glanced at Grant. Monday was only two days away. Pastor Rick worked quickly. Maybe that's how he made such a big difference.

Brook walked by, carrying a giant box filled with empty muffin tins. Sophia marched behind her with empty cardboard boxes. "I'm borrowing your daughter for a few hours," she announced. "Give me your keys. I'll grab her booster seat in the parking lot."

Sophia grinned. She dropped the boxes and gave her mom a hug. "Brook is letting me ride in the van again! I love the van. Is that okay, Mommy?"

Avery tousled her daughter's hair. "That's fine. I'm going to help Grant clean up. We'll meet you at the shop."

Brook shook her head. "Don't rush. Maybe grab a slice of pizza. The table selling hot dogs gave us lunch, but I'm sure you're hungry. I'll keep Sophia busy. Find some food and quiet time together."

Avery looked at her friend, grateful. Brook always knew when she needed a few minutes alone with Grant.

Was it always this tricky to make time with people you cared about? She wasn't sure. Eric was the first guy she'd really dated. Life was more complicated now. But in many ways, life was so much better.

With a light heart, she helped Grant fold up tables and place them against the walls. They pulled down streamers and balloon arches and emptied trash cans.

When they were done, Grant pulled her toward the door. "Let's get that pizza. I'm starving."

At the pizza place, they waited for their half-pepperoni, half-plain pie. He reached out to wrap a hand around hers across the restaurant table. She looked at their linked hands and smiled. Grant had been part of her life for a long time. Hopefully, they would be together for the rest of their lives.

Everything would work out eventually: the divorce decree, the tax money, finding a place to stay. She'd learned over the past weeks that family and friends mattered more than anything else. The rest would fall into place.

Grant gave her hand a squeeze and smiled. "What happens now?"

"I'm not sure. I have about a week to save the house or start packing. I'll talk to the bank one more time. I've got a few more weeks of steady income to show them."

"I could loan you money," he said again. "It's still an option."

She shook her head sharply. "No way. The divorce isn't even final yet. I've got to untangle the knots from one relationship before I add knots to a new one. I don't want to complicate what we have."

"I can respect that. Just don't let me be the reason you lose your house."

"If I lose the house, it won't be your fault. It's Eric's fault. I've made peace with that and moved on. But I can't run to you every time I have a problem, hoping you can solve it."

Grant shook his head, as if he didn't understand how one woman could be so stubborn. He couldn't understand. He'd never been in a relationship with someone like Eric. The next time she was part of a couple, she would be an equal partner. She would never allow someone to take over her life again.

Still, Grant didn't push the issue. He offered to help, then stepped back and let her make her own choices. Avery appreciated his thoughtfulness.

He held up his hands in defense. "I can't give you money. We're still just friends. But how can I help this week?"

Avery hesitated, feeling his warm hand on top of hers as she considered her option. It was too soon to pack up their belongings. She didn't want to scare Sophia if they could still save the house. She had one more week to move mountains for her daughter.

Looking at Grant, she came up with another plan. "No matter what happens to the house, there's still cleaning up to do. There's antique furniture to sell. It might be worth some money. And I've got an attic full of boxes. Maybe we can find some valuables up there."

She gave a silent prayer that she wasn't chasing fool's gold. They needed to clean the house, whether or not she stayed. All they needed was to find a few thousand dollars hidden under the floorboards. She chuckled to herself. That wasn't going to happen.

Grant seemed oblivious to her train of thoughts, but eager to help. "I can move furniture and help you sort things. Nick's a wizard with selling things." He sounded excited as he formed his own plan alongside Avery's. "Let's do this. The sooner, the better. Can we start tomorrow?"

"I'll make time. Call Nick and ask if he's willing to help, please. But for now, don't tell him why we're selling things. Rumors travel fast in this town. I can't let Sophia know we're in trouble."

Grant waved off her concerns with a flap of his hands. "We won't let Sophia find out why we're selling things. Besides, you're not in trouble. You're in Sunset Cove. There's no better place to be when you need help."

Chapter Twenty-Eight

Grant

Grant dropped his side of the sofa, grateful it was finally down the steps. He might work in construction, but the antique furniture was solid wood. He preferred to carry individual pieces of wood before he nailed them into place, thank you very much.

He couldn't believe Avery's furniture was this heavy. Not that he'd complain to Avery, of course. He would do everything in his power to help save her childhood home.

Nick sat down on the sofa, catching his breath. He caressed the intricately carved armrest. "It's heavy, but it's beautiful. This should be worth a pretty penny at the mall's antique shop."

Grant groaned as he thought of dragging the sofa out to his truck and into town. It had been hard enough to move it downstairs. "Do you have an appointment with the shop? Or are you sending pictures?"

"I'm one step ahead of you." Nick waved his phone at Grant. He chuckled and gave his friend a mischievous grin. "I took pictures before we moved it. I've got texts out to three different people: the shop owner, the local historical society, and a private collector. They're aware they're bidding against each other. That might help drive up the price."

Grant reached out to give Nick a fist bump. Calling Nick had been the right decision, even if he didn't know why they were selling furniture.

Nick was always the first person on-site when they did a house demolition or reconstruction, salvaging antiques and helping owners choose new furnishings. He had a real eye for it.

Grant was glad Nick cared enough to help. Avery needed every dollar, of course. But even without knowing about the tax bill, Nick understood the struggle of single moms. His own wife had raised a child alone before they were married.

It was funny how things came full circle. He'd thought Nick was crazy for taking on Jessica and her son. Jessica was great, but at the time he couldn't imagine loving a stepson as your own.

Then Avery came back into his life, and he met Sophia. He loved them both fiercely. It still shocked him how simple it had been.

Grant grinned when Avery came down the steps covered in dust. She carried a box filled with plates, cups, and saucers. "These might not be worth much." She gently placed the box at Nick's feet. "You don't use china in construction. Furniture is more of your thing. Could you ask your contacts if they'd be interested in this, too?"

Nick nodded, but glanced between the plates and Avery with a look of concern on his face. "Are these special to you? I don't want to sell things you aren't ready to get rid of."

Avery shook her head and smiled. "They could be some antiques Grandpa bought at an auction. I don't know where they're from, so I have no attachment to them. I'm keeping the things I remember my grandfather using."

Nick pulled out his phone and took a picture, then did an image search on the internet. He let out a low whistle. "You're sure you want to sell these? They might be rare. They're valuable, in any case."

Avery let out a sigh of relief. "Good. I was hoping they'd be worth something. Yes, I'm sure I want to sell them."

"Let me contact some people. Let's see how many bidding wars we can start in one day." He grinned, typing a quick message out on his phone.

"Nick has devoted the day to causing a county-wide bidding war," Grant said. He patted the sofa next to him and hoped Avery would rest for a minute. "He's determined to get top dollar. Your antiques are in excellent hands."

Avery nodded and stared at the floor carpet. Concerned, Grant tugged her hand until she sat next to him. It must be hard to tear apart your house, hoping to raise enough money to save it.

He'd had enough money struggles growing up. His mom had stopped working for long periods while she was sick. Somehow, they'd always gotten by. They hadn't needed to sell belongings to make ends meet.

His heart went out to Avery. He eased his arm over her shoulders and squeezed her in a sideways hug. "It's going to be okay. None of these sales are final until you've got a check. We can stop at any time."

Avery leaned closer and snuggled on his shoulder. "We can't stop. No matter what happens, this stuff has to go." She sat up and gave him a smile. "I'll be fine, just feeling a little regret. It doesn't matter if we get rid of this stuff. I wish my grandfather was here to help me sort through it."

Grant gave her another squeeze, starting to understand. The past year had been tough. She'd lost her grandfather and her marriage. Now she might lose her home. But to his surprise, she continued to smile.

"This is big, isn't it? No matter what happens over the next few weeks, I'll have my fresh start. Besides, I don't even like this couch. I want furniture Sophia can use. We'll keep our old, comfy recliner. I want to put my feet up, and I'm not doing it on antique furniture."

Nick turned the phone around to show off his latest text. "My collector will pay two hundred dollars for the plates and cups. I think he's crazy, but it's your stuff. Should we wait to see if someone offers more?"

Avery's eyes widened as she looked into the box at their feet. It wasn't even a big box. There were less than a dozen plates and cups. If Nick's friend was willing to pay two hundred dollars for it, she wouldn't argue.

Grant laughed and gave Avery another squeeze. "I told you Nick is a wizard. Let's see how much he gets for this enormous sofa."

· ♥ · ♥ · ♥ · ♥ · ♥ ·

Eight hours later, they wrapped up phase one of Operation Clean Slate. Nick had a list of agreed prices and pickup times for the antique furniture in the house, including her grandparents' bedroom suite. They weren't using his room or any of its furniture. She slept in the guest room, while Sophia used her old childhood room.

Avery stopped them from selling her grandfather's office desk, though. He was glad she'd found a limit.

Nick had worked hard all day, helping them pull out furniture and dig through boxes in the attic. He'd searched the internet to see what might be valuable. It was worth it. Together, they'd earned thousands of dollars. Grant shook his head as he looked through Nick's list. The antique store would send a delivery truck tomorrow to pick up the biggest furniture. Nick's private collector had come and gone, taking the plates, a stack of vintage records, and more, leaving behind a few hundred dollars in cash.

"I can't thank you enough," Avery gushed again. "You were both a huge help. I couldn't have done this so quickly by myself."

Nick shoved his hands into his coat pocket and nodded. "It's no problem. We'll be here in the morning to help load the furniture. Can I do anything else before I leave? Jessica's waiting for me, but I can give you a few more minutes."

Avery looked around the room and shook her head. "We've done everything we can. Go home. Thank Jessica for letting us borrow you."

Nick laughed as he walked out the door.

Grant looked around the room one last time, taking in the groups of furniture and a few boxes filled with vintage clothes. "We did good. Don't you think so?"

"We did great. I can't believe Nick sold all of this in one day."

"The man has connections. He works with the local antique shop and a few other people during remodeling jobs. Sometimes he'll spend an hour in his truck, looking for the perfect lighting fixture on his phone. The customers love him."

"Are you sure he isn't playing Candy Crush?"

"He might be. But he gets the job done," Grant said, chuckling. The laughter faded as he looked at Avery with a serious look. He'd promised he wouldn't bug Avery about the tax bill. It was none of his business. But even if they weren't dating yet, they were still best friends. He needed to know. "It's a lot of money. But is it enough?"

She sighed and walked into the kitchen. She pulled out two mugs and added some coffee to the machine, avoiding his eyes. As the coffeemaker sputtered to life, she turned to Grant with a sad smile. "It's close. We're getting close."

"How close?"

"A lot closer than we were yesterday," she said, avoiding his gaze once again. "I'll go through the attic and my grandfather's office one last time. Hopefully Nick doesn't mind. I might text him more pictures."

"We're all friends. He won't mind."

"Then let's forget about that for now." She walked into the kitchen and pulled out two mugs from the cabinets, speaking over her shoulder while she worked. "Do you still like sugar with your coffee?"

He shook his head, surprised that she remembered. "I started drinking it black a few years ago. I don't have time to hunt for sugar on the job."

"Smart. I am a tired mother who works in a bakery. I'll take my sugar where I can find it. Sophia should be home soon, and I'm going to need the energy." She poured herself a generous dollop of cream and added a spoonful of sugar.

The friends leaned against the kitchen counter, sipping their drinks in silence. Grant glanced around the kitchen, hoping this wouldn't be the last time they shared coffee here. It seemed like just yesterday he'd burst through that front door, eager to grab a snack from Clint Brown's cookie jar before he did homework with Avery.

As if on cue, the door burst open and Sophia flew into the living room. "Mommy! Where are you? Why are there so many chairs?"

"We're in the kitchen! Be right there," Avery called out. Then she turned to Grant and smiled. "Thanks for the company. I'm back on Mom duty again."

Grant watched as his friend placed her coffee mug in the sink and headed out to greet her daughter. He wondered how much energy it cost her to keep up a cheerful face. It was hard enough to worry about the future; it must be doubly difficult to hide those worries from your child.

He rinsed out his own mug and walked toward the living room. While Avery was pasting on a fake smile for her daughter while she explained why their "fancy furniture" was downstairs, he didn't need to fake it. Just listening to the little girl's chatter made him grin.

He stood in the doorway as Avery explained they were getting rid of the furniture they didn't use. Sophia took it in stride, tracing her finger along the carved wood of the sofa before she flopped onto their old recliner with a sigh.

"Can we make the library into a playroom? Kendra has a playroom next to her bedroom, and it's filled with games and toys. She has a table to make crafts. It's great!" Sophia bounced up and down in her chair. "If we had somewhere to play, I could invite her over! She hasn't seen our house yet."

Grant glanced at Avery and saw the hurt on her face. She quickly hid the hurt with another fake smile. "We'll see what happens. This sofa was taking up a lot of space, but the library isn't empty yet."

He quietly picked up his coat and prepared to leave, sensing that Avery needed this time alone with her daughter. It had been a long day. She put on a brave face, but it couldn't be easy watching people buy your childhood memories.

Grant gave her a nod as he shrugged on his coat. He wanted to give her a big hug and sneak another kiss, but not in front of Sophia. There were too many changes happening right now. It was best for Avery to make the first move. "Will you be at Monday's meeting?"

Avery's blank face told him she'd already forgotten. "What meeting?"

"We both agreed to be on the Kindness Committee board. We're going over the fundraiser and planning our next project. I can pick you up at six."

Sophia cheered and grabbed her mother's arm. "Can I sleep over at Kendra's house again? Pleeeease? Emma said I could. She can take me to school in the morning."

Avery slid her arm out of her daughter's grasp and around her shoulders instead. She gave her a hug and smiled. Grant was happy to see that this smile looked genuine. "Let me talk to Emma, okay? But if it's fine with her, it's okay with me."

Grant walked out the door, wishing more than ever that he didn't need to leave his two girls.

Chapter Twenty-Nine

Avery

Avery paced the floor of her living room, not sure what to do with herself. Emma had left with her daughter a few minutes ago; Grant would be here in ten minutes to pick her up for their meeting.

It gave her a few minutes to think. She glanced around the room one last time. Avery didn't want to admit it, but she was scared.

She'd sold a bunch of furniture, and found a few more collectibles in her grandfather's office. She'd taken out the line of credit on her new credit card. Her brother had done the same, and yet they were still a thousand dollars away from paying off the tax bill. One thousand dollars didn't seem like a lot of money, but she was scraping the bottom of the barrel. It might as well be a million dollars.

She'd turned down loans from both of her friends. Her divorce would be finalized soon, and she was ready to start a relationship with Grant. He'd waited so patiently. He deserved a clean slate with her, not a relationship complicated by money.

Avery wasn't leaving. But she didn't know how she could afford to stay.

What a mess.

Still, pacing the floors wouldn't solve any problems. Avery needed to set her worries aside for a few hours and focus on the Kindness Committee and Grant. She would help this town to the best of her ability, and soon she could love Grant freely.

The feeling she had for Grant grew stronger every day, especially when he acted so kind and gentle with her daughter. He would make a great dad.

Avery sighed and when out to the porch to wait for Grant. She locked the door behind her as his truck rolled up to the sidewalk. That was Grant: always punctual. He wouldn't want to be late or hold up the meeting.

She shook her head. How had she ever thought Eric was the man for her? Her ex-husband hadn't thought about anyone but himself.

Grant jumped out of the truck and opened the passenger side door. He leaned in to give her a quick kiss on the cheek. Her mood brightened as she gave him a quick grin. They were both eager for her divorce to be final.

He smoothly closed the door, slid into his own seat, and pulled out onto the empty road. "We're a few minutes early. Let's grab coffee for everyone," he suggested. A few minutes later, they found a local coffee shop that was still open and ordered a large thermos of coffee.

It wasn't an expensive treat, but it was a thoughtful surprise. She smiled to herself as he mentioned one of their members was diabetic and needed artificial sweetener. Grant always thought of other people.

She helped him carry in the thermos, cups, and everything else they would need. Then she settled at the conference table next to Grant and watched people walk in.

Harry was soon there. The silver-haired man was a regular at the meetings, and he gave Avery a wink as he entered the room.

To her surprise, Pastor Rick stood talking to Brook. Her best friend hadn't mentioned she was joining the board, but it was good to see her here.

Pastor Rick stood to lead the group in prayer to start the meeting. Together, they prayed for guidance and to understand their path as they strived to build a stronger community.

The pastor smiled warmly at the dozen people gathered around the table and handed out an agenda. "Let's get started. I've put together a list of projects. We'll discuss each project, how much it costs, and a timeline. Take notes. After we've discussed these projects, we're going to vote on them. I'd like our votes to be confidential. I suggest we don't spend all our money at this meeting. Some of these projects will take time to complete, and we want our money to last until the next fundraiser."

Avery nodded thoughtfully as her eyes roamed through the list. He was right, of course. Money was tight for everyone. Even though they'd raised thousands of dollars, they couldn't do everything. If they fixed one person's roof for ten thousand dollars, they wouldn't be able to do as many smaller projects. It would be a tough choice, deciding if they needed to do one big project or lots of smaller projects.

She paused at the end of the list. Most of the items had names and addresses attached to them. But the last two lines had no name or location attached; they simply said "sick child" and "single mom." Both would cost five hundred dollars.

The pastor went down the list, explaining each project. A teacher at Sunset Cove Elementary was requesting ten winter coats for kids at the school. The local library was expanding their children's section, and someone had suggested a "kindness box" at the library filled with children's books and snacks. The food pantry needed a second freezer.

So many people in the community had suggested ways to help others. Avery found it overwhelming, but also comforting. She wasn't alone in her struggles. The town's people would work through their troubles by working together.

Pastor Rick continued through the list until he reached the bottom. "Two requests don't have names attached to them. I've been asked to respect the privacy of these two families. We've got a young child in our congregation who will need surgery, and her parents need money for food and gas while they travel back and forth to Children's Hospital of Philadelphia. They haven't told many people yet. Both parents are taking time off work, so money will be tight."

The people around the table nodded, and Avery wrote a small "yes" next to that item. She knew how tough it was to lose your income and still care for a child.

"The second donation we'll vote on is a single mom in Sunset Cove. She's facing housing issues through no fault of her own, and this money would give her family some stability."

Avery nodded again and wrote "yes" on her agenda. Warm clothes, food, and stability were all gifts she could support.

Pastor Rick walked around the room, handing out another piece of paper for the vote. "You can vote 'yes,' 'no,' or 'not now.' For a project to happen, we need a simple majority. Good luck. We've got some tough choices to make tonight."

Avery silently agreed. There were tough choices to make. She immediately checked "not now" for the roof repairs. It was an important project, but it cost too much.

The coats, freezer, and sick child were an easy "yes," but she hesitated as she considered the single mom's housing issues. They sounded a lot like her own struggles. She knew how much her own problems were weighing her down, and how hard she was fighting to give Sophia stability.

How would she vote if it was her own daughter? Or Emma? Of course she would vote "yes." Every family deserved a stable home, and she would do whatever she could to support local families—even while her own family was struggling.

She folded her paper in half and passed it forward with the rest of the votes. Pastor Rick moved to the whiteboard, where he quickly tallied the votes. It didn't surprise her to see the biggest project, the roof, voted down for now. The group approved all the smaller ideas. They could even help the two unnamed families and stay well within their budget.

Pastor Rick looked pleased as he finished circling the approved projects. "Great job, everyone. There are twelve of us, and fifteen projects for this winter. I want each of you to volunteer for at least two projects. You'll be in charge of the details. That means completing tasks, finding helpers at our general meetings, or asking local businesses to donate their time and supplies."

Avery immediately raised her hand. "I can buy the coats if you have clothing sizes. And I'll help the two unnamed families."

He nodded and scrawled Avery's name next to both projects. She sat back, pleased. She might not have her life completely under control, but it felt good to help other families in need.

Each board member added their name to a few projects. They even suggested ways to make the "not now" projects happen for no cost. Grant would check out the roof that needed to be replaced; he hoped to patch any leaks before winter with his own supplies.

Pastor Rick wrapped up the meeting after asking the committee members to report back in two weeks with updates on their projects. "Avery, I'd like to deliver a check to the hospitalized family tomorrow. Can I pick you up after work?" he asked.

She thought about her schedule and nodded. "Sophia will be at school, so that's fine. I'm happy to help."

She walked out of the meeting with Grant, then slid into his truck and let out a sigh.

He slid into his own seat and gave her a wry smile. "That was tough, wasn't it? Choosing who to help, I mean. I didn't expect it to be so hard."

"It *was* hard," she agreed. "I thought it would be simple. We raise money and spend it. I didn't realize how many people needed help in this town. It makes my own problems seem so insignificant."

Grant waved her off and started his truck, pulling onto the road and heading toward her house. "Your problems are as important as anyone else's. To be honest, I wanted to ask if we could help you, too. We all want you to stay in Sunset Cove."

She sighed again and ran a hand through her hair. It was a frizzy mess by the end of most days. Despite all the worries she had in her life, she wished she'd looked nicer for Grant.

She shook off that thought and smiled at him as he opened the truck door. "Do you want to come inside? Sophia is at her sleepover. I've got some chocolate chip cookies from the bakery."

"Cookies sound like a great way to end the night."

Avery dropped her purse on the counter, then spun around to face Grant. "Just let me grab the mail. I didn't have time to fetch it earlier."

Grant shook his head. "Get the cookies ready. I'll get the mail."

Avery busied herself with the tray of cookies left over from this morning's baking. She got out plates and set them on the kitchen table, then poured two small glasses of milk.

She blushed as she realized this was the first time they'd been truly alone. Sophia wouldn't be home anytime soon. When Grant came in with the mail, an awkward silence stretched between them.

Desperate to remain calm, Avery started chattering. "I hope you don't mind whole milk. Sophia says anything else tastes funny, so I buy what she likes. Are we too old for milk and cookies? It seemed like a better idea than nightcaps. I don't drink."

"Milk and cookies are the perfect way to end the night," he said. "As long as I'm with you, everything is perfect."

The fear around her heart melted. This man was perfect. Why didn't she realize this years ago?

Grant pretended to stagger under the weight of the mail, then grinned at her as he handed it over. "It looks like you haven't got to the mailbox in a few days. I almost dropped it all, pulling it out of the box."

Avery nodded and absentmindedly shifted through the envelopes. "It's been a few days," she agreed. "I've been caught up in other things. Eric handled the mail and I'm getting into the habit of doing it myself. I'm expecting a letter from..."

She stuttered to a stop as she flipped to an envelope from her lawyer. Should she open it now, or should she wait until Grant was gone? She wasn't sure if the letter was related to the divorce.

Grant seemed to sense the mood change. He picked up a cookie and bit into it, carefully catching the crumbs in his hand. "These cookies are great. Are you sure you want me to stay, though? You could catch up on the mail while Sophia is gone."

Avery looked at the man who had her been her best friend for years. Did she need privacy? Or was it time to let Grant into her life?

After thinking it over for a few seconds, she shook her head. "It's fine. No matter what's in this envelope, I'll tell you about it. You might as well be here when I open it."

She put the rest of the mail down and slid a finger under the envelope flap. She ripped it open and pulled out the paper inside, holding it with trembling hands.

After scanning the paper, she smiled. "It's not about the house. It doesn't fix any of my money problems. But as of two days ago, I'm officially free. Eric signed the papers. We finalized the divorce."

Grant closed the last few feet between them. He took the paper out of her hand and let it drift onto the kitchen table, then pulled her into his arms and held her tightly. She squeezed her eyes shut, holding back the tears that threatened to fall. She wasn't grieving the end of her marriage. These were tears of joy.

Grant pulled away and looked into Avery's eyes. "How do you feel?"

"I feel... Free. Like I'm finally ready for that second chance."

He continued to search her eyes, as if looking for answers to questions he hadn't asked yet. "Do you think I'll be part of a second chance?"

"I hope so."

"Are you ready for us?"

Avery worried she was rushing things, but was she really? It was like they'd picked up where they'd left off, all those years ago. Looking back, she'd been ready to date Grant for ages.

She grinned and squeezed his hand. "I'm ready when you are."

He threaded his hands into her curly hair and slowly drew her closer. He kissed her with a passion that had her tingling from head to toe, silently sharing the frustration and longing they'd felt over the last few weeks.

When they finally broke apart, Grant leaned over and rested his forehead on hers. "I was a fool. I should have done that ten years ago when I had the chance."

"It wasn't the right time. Maybe you needed a second chance, too."

Grant twisted his lips as if he was considering the idea. "I like that. No regrets this time. I'm all in. How about you?"

"I'm all in, too. I might not get to keep this house, but I'm keeping you."

Grant threw his head back and roared with laughter. "I'm all yours, woman. I've been yours for years. Will you let me help with the house now?"

Avery shook her head again. "No. This is my problem, and while you're part of my life, I won't drag anyone else into my problems. If we lose the house, I'll use the money for a down payment somewhere else. We'll make it work. It's a roof and four walls. We'll find another roof to live under."

Grant sighed. "It's just a roof, but think about all the memories you have here. I don't want you to lose that."

"I've got a few more days. I haven't given up yet," she said.

Chapter Thirty

Avery

Avery's heart felt like it might burst with joy when she walked into the bakery on Tuesday morning.

Grant had left after he finished his milk and cookies. She was grateful he hadn't pressured her to move too quickly. Hopefully, they'd be seeing a lot more of each other.

The bakery door's bell jingled cheerfully. She walked into the kitchen to see Brook hunched over a gigantic pile of dough.

Her friend grinned and grabbed a towel to wipe off her hands. Her eyes sparkled mischievously. "You're here. I thought you would sleep in after all the excitement last night. How late did you stay up with Grant?"

Avery grabbed an apron to protect her clothes and swatted Brook playfully. "You know me better than that. He was gone by nine o'clock. I was asleep thirty minutes later. I couldn't miss the chance to go to bed early."

Brook shook her head and attacked the dough again. "I'm disappointed in you. You're the only one of us with a chance at an interesting story, and you choose an early bedtime."

"It's too soon. I just got divorced yesterday."

Brook's eyes widened. "Wait. Is it finally official? Are you finally free from Eric?" Brook gave the dough an enthusiastic punch as she said her ex-husband's name.

"I am officially Miss Avery Brown again." She pumped her hands in the air, then paused. "At least, I will be. I have to change my name at the courthouse."

Brook squealed and wrapped her friend in a flour-filled hug. "I'm so excited for you. You deserve this second chance. Oh, look at me. I'm getting flour everywhere." She stepped back and brushed her hands off again with a towel. "I have your paycheck ready. You forgot to pick it up yesterday."

Brook picked up a sealed envelope and handed it to her friend. Avery did a double-take as she peeked inside the envelope. "This isn't right. This can't be my paycheck."

"Of course it is. That includes all the overtime you worked during last week, plus twenty percent of the profits from the Lighthouse festival. I couldn't have done it without your help."

Avery was nearly speechless. "But.... No. There's more than a thousand dollars extra. This can't be right."

"It was a very successful sale, thanks to you. I brought twice the number of baked goods that I usually do, and I sold it all. You deserve a cut."

Avery stared at her friend for a moment, then walked over to the kitchen stool and collapsed onto the chair.

Brook rushed over, forgetting the dough. "Are you okay? I wanted to pay back everything you've done for me. You've been a big help. The bakery is growing, thanks to you. We might even expand soon."

"It's not that. I'm glad to help, and I'm grateful for the job. But do you realize how much this money means?"

"It's been a tough month. I wish I could give more, but I hope this will help."

Avery stared at the check. Her eyes overflowed with tears. "You don't understand. With this extra money, I can pay off the taxes on our house."

Brook dragged over her own stool and jumped onto the seat. "Were you that close? Why didn't you say anything? I could have given you this bonus weeks ago."

Avery wiped the tears out of her eyes, marveling at how everything had fallen together.

Her pay from the lighthouse festival was the last of the money she needed, but she couldn't have done it without all of her friends' help. Grant had moved furniture and carried collectibles from the attic. Nick had found buyers for her antiques. And her grandfather had left her a home in a community so filled with love and kindness that she'd fought until the end to stay.

She was staying in Sunset Cove. Her heart leaped as she realized she'd accomplished the impossible. Her grandfather's tax bill would be paid. Avery wouldn't need to pull Sophia out of school and away from her new friends. She wouldn't need to build a relationship with Grant from another town. With this last bit of money, she could start over with a clean slate.

Avery stood on shaky legs to wrap her friend in a warm hug. "Thank you for everything. For being my friend when I didn't deserve it, and for giving me a job that I love. I won't let you down."

Brook gave her friend a gentle squeeze back. "I know you won't let me down. You're finally growing roots in Sunset Cove. They look good on you. Now let's get to work. This bread won't bake itself."

· ♥ · ♥ · ♥ · ♥ · ♥ ·

A few hours later, Avery found herself in Pastor Rick's car, headed to the local hospital. They'd meet the family with a sick child there and surprise them with the Kindness Committee's check.

He updated her while they drove. "The girl's name is Olivia. They diagnosed her with acute lymphoblastic leukemia last week. She's staying at Sunset County Medical Center until she can transfer to CHOP. Her prognosis is good, but the family has a long journey ahead of them. They're private people. Please don't tell anyone else about this visit."

"No, of course not. How old is she?"

"She's three. Her parents are young, too. They're in their early twenties. It's been a lot for them to handle. I'm guessing they'll relate better to another young parent, which is why I asked you to come along."

Avery stared out the window as the forest between Sunset Cove and the hospital pass them by. Her heart broke for the little girl. Avery couldn't imagine Sophia dealing with something like this, and prayed that she never would.

The next hour was humbling. They scrubbed their arms and sanitized to prevent spreading germs to the young patient, then spent time with Olivia's parents while their daughter slept.

Olivia's parents were grateful for the money and even more grateful for the company. They were alone in Sunset County, with no family and few friends to support them.

Avery pulled a paper out of her purse and scrawled out her name and phone number. "Call me anytime. I used to live in Philadelphia, so I'm familiar with the area. If you need anything, even a shoulder to cry on, let me know."

Olivia was still sleeping when they left. Except for the tubes and wires attached to her hands and chest, she looked like a healthy little girl. She still had a full head of hair. Her dad explained they were keeping her stable at the medical center. The real treatment and all of its side effects would start once they got to CHOP.

When Avery walked out of the hospital with Pastor Rick, he led them to a bench near the entrance.

"Thank you for coming. You've given those parents a real lifeline. It's hard enough to be a parent. Imagine trying to parent through an illness."

"I hope I was helpful. I can't imagine what they're going through."

He nodded thoughtfully, then turned to look at Avery as she stared at the sidewalk. "I hope this means you're staying in Sunset Cove. As you saw today, we could use people like you on the Kindness board."

Despite the last tear streaking down her face, Avery broke into a wide grin. "Yes, we're staying. Everything worked out."

Pastor Rick cheered and gripped her hand. "I'm so glad. Have you told Grant yet?"

"Not yet. I just finalized our plans this morning, and I didn't want to interrupt his day. We invited him over for pizza tonight. I was going to tell him after we put Sophia to bed."

He shook his head and pulled her toward the car. "Why are we still here? Go tell Grant the good news. He won't mind the interruption."

A few minutes later, Pastor Rick dropped her off at the O'Neill house. It had been an enormous project, but the crew was nearly done. Looking up at the house, Avery couldn't help thinking of her own problems. There'd been a lot to tackle, but she'd worked through it, one day at a time.

Avery knocked on the door and let herself into the house. Grant was in the living room tacking down the carpeting. His face lit up when he saw her. He dropped the hammer and rushed to her side.

"Avery! What are you doing here? Is something wrong?"

"Everything is great. Am I interrupting you?"

He leaned in and gave her a slow kiss that made her head spin. "You're never interrupting me. I could use a break, anyway."

Grant led her through the living room and into the kitchen, where new cabinets and countertops gleamed. He poured two cups of lukewarm coffee out of a thermos and gestured toward the table. Instead of sitting down, Avery took the cup and grinned, leaning against the counter.

"I'm going to the tax office today to pay off my grandfather's bill. I thought you'd want to know."

Grant grabbed the coffee mug from her hand and slid both mugs onto the counter. Then he lifted her off the ground in an enormous hug. When he finally put her down, his smile stretched from ear to ear. He reached around his back to unhook his tool belt.

"That's worth the interruption! When do we leave?"

"What do you mean? Are you coming too?"

"Sure, if you don't mind. It's a big step. I'd like to support you."

Avery closed her eyes for a moment, trying to hold back tears. Despite being married, she'd been so lonely over the past few years. She said a silent prayer of thanks that Grant was back in her life.

"I'd like that. We can leave whenever you're ready."

Epilogue

"Brad, can you pull the turkey out of the oven?"

Avery watched her brother wrestle a twenty-five pound turkey onto the stovetop. She might have gone overboard for their first Thanksgiving, but it was an important holiday, and her first family gathering in more than a decade in Sunset Cove.

Her family had grown well beyond her brother and daughter. Grant was part of her family now. Brook and her other friends were like family, too. While this wouldn't be the "single girls" Thanksgiving they'd planned, her new friends were happy for her. She was grateful to have so many loved ones under one roof.

Brad groaned as put his hand on his back and stretched. "You're killing me. Doesn't your boyfriend pick up heavy things for a living?"

Avery just laughed. "You work in construction, too. One turkey shouldn't bother either of you. Grant and Sophia ran down to the bakery to help Brook with the pies. You want pie, right?"

"I'll eat anything Brook makes. She was a fantastic baker in high school. Hopefully nothing's changed."

Avery swatted him with a dish towel and nested foil over the turkey. "You ate enough of her cookies and pies, didn't you? She was always experimenting at our house and sending leftovers back to your dorm."

Her big brother had come home from college more often once Brook started baking at their house. Sometimes she wondered if he came for the pie or for Brook. Still, the two of them had never moved beyond friendship.

As if reading her mind, Brad kept the conversation focused on Brook. "How's she doing? I heard she opened a bakery, but never had time to stop by."

"She's doing well. We work together now, but you know that. This meal was her idea. We planned it for single women only, but they were happy to let you and Grant join in the fun."

He raised an eyebrow and considered what she'd said. "Brook's still single, huh?"

Avery gave her brother a mischievous grin and handed him a heavy stack of plates to put on the table. "She's still single. What's it to you?"

He shrugged as he slid each plate into place, looking uncomfortable. He moved back to the drawer to pull out silverware and continued setting the table. "She's like a sister to me. I would feel weird asking her out."

"It's funny. Grant said the same thing in high school. He doesn't think dating me is weird anymore."

"And look at you now. A ring on your finger and...." He rushed over to the oven and pulled the door open. "There's no bun in the oven. Too soon?"

Avery held her hand out, admiring her engagement ring. Grant hadn't wasted time. After waiting years to find their way to each other, they were eager to start a new life together. "Of course it's too soon. The wedding isn't for a few more months. One step at a time."

"I'm ready for another niece or nephew. I love chaos."

"Have your own kids if you like them. Find a nice girl and settle down. But speaking of chaos...." She paused and cocked her ear toward the front door.

A moment later, Sophia threw open the door and flew into the room, a cold breeze following her. She set a paper bag on the counter and ran into her mother's arms. "I have cookies! Dad has the pies. And Brook says she's supervising because it's her day off."

Avery grinned. Sophia had gotten her wish; Grant's new name was "Dad." She felt lucky to find a man who could be a father to Sophia. Grant was living in his own house until they were married, but spent more time with Sophia than her ex-husband ever did.

Grant walked in after their daughter, juggling a half-dozen pies. "I bring dessert, and one baker taking the day off." He set the pies on the counter and wrapped his arms around Avery. She put a hand on his chest to stop him from more than a peck on the lips.

After pausing for a quick kiss, she watched Brad and Sophia race into the living room. Sophia squealed with delight. "Welcome to the crazy house," Avery said.

"It's only going to get better. Emma's bringing her daughter, remember? Uncle Brad should have plenty of kids to play with." Grant grinned as he snuck his hand into the paper bag and snagged a handful of cookies.

Brook swatted his hand. "Those are for after dinner. Don't spoil your appetite."

Avery shook her head and smiled while the two of them bickered. Nothing had changed since high school. She was grateful they'd both accepted her back into their lives. She'd returned to Sunset Cove alone and out of options. Now she was living in her grandfather's home, surrounded by loved ones.

After everyone had arrived, Brook wrangled their friends and children into the living room. They'd expanded the table and wedged in enough chairs for everyone, but it was a tight fit. Brook immediately took charge, ushering people into chairs.

When there were a few empty chairs left, Avery noticed an awkward shuffle happening in the back corner. It seemed like Brad was trying not to sit next to Brook. Interesting. She wondered what that was about.

She held back a giggle as Brad pulled out a chair for Brook, then cleared his throat. He dashed away from the empty chair next to her, sitting next to his niece instead.

Her brother was staying in Sunset Cove until spring—there would be plenty of time to see how this played out. Avery settled into the seat between Sophia and Grant, trying to hide a grin as she considered her brother's awkwardness.

Her daughter beamed. "We should give thanks. You give thanks on Thanksgiving!" She reached out to hold her mother's and uncle's hands, and everyone around the table followed her lead. Then Sophia leaned forward and whispered, "What do I do now?"

Grant chuckled and whispered back, "I've got this, kiddo."

He squeezed Avery's hand and raised his voice. "We have a lot to be thankful for this year. I want to give thanks for my friends, and the new family we're building. We consider all of you to be part of our family now. I hope you'll think the same."

Sophia giggled. "We have a big family! I like having a big family. Can we eat now?"

Her uncle reached for a piece of turkey, sliding the first slice onto Sophia's plate. "Let's get started."

Yes, let's get started, Avery thought. *I'm ready to start my new life.*

·♥·♥·♥·♥·♥·

Ready for more Sunset Cove? Read Brook and Brad's story (and finish Avery and Grant's wedding journey) in *Second Chances in Sunset Cove*.

She doesn't give second chances. He'd do anything to prove he's changed. Will sparks fly when these former friends are forced to work together?

Brook Reed knows that when a man treats you poorly, it's time to walk away. That's why it hurt so badly when her friend Brad Brown disappeared after their first date—no calls, no texts, and no explanations. Now he's in charge of her bakery expansion, and she'll be at Brad's side during his sister's small-town wedding.

Brad isn't proud of his speed-dating reputation. He's changed since disappearing from Brook's life, and no other woman has come close to capturing his heart. When he moves back to his childhood home in Sunset Cove, Brad discovers how much he's lost by running from family and responsibilities. He'll do anything to prove that he's a better man now, and the right man for Brook.

When a storm threatens his sister's wedding and the residents of Sunset Cove, Brook and Brad will be pushed together yet again. Can they overcome the past to claim their last chance at happiness?

Read the second book in this sweet, small-town beach series now!

Free Short Story

Avery and Grant's engagement story is now available, and it's exclusive to newsletter subscribers!

Sign up for Tori Mitchell's monthly newsletter at subscribepage.io/ToriMitchell to get a free copy of *Forever Home in Sunset Cove*. You'll be the first to know about upcoming books, discounts, and more.

Join the Kindness Committee!

Thank you for reading *Coming Home to Sunset Cove*. If you enjoyed Grant and Avery's story, please consider leaving a review on Amazon or Goodreads. Even a short review can help us reach new readers and spread more kindness.

How does a story spread kindness? **If you purchased this book, you've officially joined the Sunset Cove Kindness Committee!** Ten percent of profits from the Sunset Cove series are donated to non-profit organizations like the Child Life program at Children's Hospital of Philadelphia, which helps children facing a serious illness or hospitalization.

About the Author

Tori Mitchell writes sweet, small-town romance with a guaranteed Happily Ever After.

She found her own small-town happy ending in the Pocono Mountains of Pennsylvania, where she lives with her husband and two children. When she's not reading, writing or daydreaming about the beach, you'll find Tori growing an absurd amount of tomatoes and rhubarb in her garden.

Get the latest news on sales, new books, and more with Tori's newsletter at subscribepage.io/ToriMitchellnewsletter.

Printed in Great Britain
by Amazon